APOLOGY FROM ONE SISTA' TO ANOTHER

A Novel

Author: Shywanee L. Manson

Apology From One Sista' To Another
Copyright 2003 by Shywanee L. Manson

All rights reserved.
No part of this book may be reproduced, stored in a retrieval system, or transmitted by any means, electronic, mechanical, photocopying, recording, or otherwise, without written permission from the author. This novel is a work of fiction. Names, characters, places and incidents either are creations from the author's imagination or used fictitiously. Any resemblance to actual persons, living or dead, events or places is entirely coincidental.

For information or to provide your feedback about this book, you may contact author at:

shyfox74@aol.com

ACKNOWLEGEMENTS

First and foremost, I want to thank my Lord and Savior, JESUS CHRIST for everything that HE has done for me. I thank HIM for the good and the bad times. Without the up and downs in my life, I would never know the true meaning of a blessing. Thank you Heavenly Father!

I'd like to thank my mother, Paula Manson, and grandmother, Delores Manson, for always being supportive and always pushing me to go forth with my goals. Without you two, I don't know how I would have turned out ☺. You are my two favorite women in the world. I love you both very much! Thank you for doing a great job of keeping me in my place and making sure I stayed on the right path.

Thanks to my two beautiful children, Stirling Manson and Shyanne Bates who make every day worth living. I love you guys with all of my heart, mind and soul. You are my everything! I dedicated all of my accomplishments in life to you. And everything that I do in life, I do for you. Thank you for being such sweet children and making your mother the happiest and proudest mother in the world.

Thanks to all of my brothers (Charles Blackhawk, Brian Roberts, Rashad Manson), sisters (Jacqualene Manson, Tiffany Manson, Sharita Roberts, Sophia Manson, Bernice Moses), cousins (to name a few, Mokadi Manson, Shineeka Manson, Kenya Manson, Marcellus Norwood, Gregory Reynolds, Raymont Reynolds, Racine Reynolds, Stephanie Monroe, Richard Monroe, Amanda Manson, Devina Manson, David Manson, Michael Manson, Mariah and Kayla), uncles (Paul Manson, Alan Manson, Keith Manson, Jandl Manson, Robert Herron and Darryl Manson), aunts (Pauline Monroe, Vicki Manson,

Beverly Funchus, Debra Herron), who make every holiday and gathering "special in our own little way". I love you all! Thanks to all of my nieces and nephews for being so sweet to auntie! I love all of you guys! (Pariesse, Charles Jr., Maurice, Wesley, Judy, Missy, Ishmal, Ashanti, Janarius, Quiana, Raquia, Tyrese, Brian Jr., Yasmine, Alyssa, Neihmaya, Sierra and Antwon Jr.).

I'd like to thank the love of my life and best friend, Terrell Westbrook, for being patient and standing by me through thick and thin. I can always depend on you to be there for me. You are a good man and I'll always love you. I appreciate all that you do for me and my children.

Thanks to my book club, "Sisters In Thought" for showing me what real friends are made of. You ladies are one of the highlights of my life and I look forward to us getting together every month. (Yolanda Sykes, Cassandra (Butter) Curtis, Pat Petersen, Verneada Greer, Debbie Abina, Tammye Coleman, Serena Smith, Lushanda Meachum, Renitta Jacobs, Bonnie McDuffie, Jo Stafford, Cherise Sneed, Katherine Tyson, Zelbra Cotton and Yolanda (Lan) Brown). Thanks for your support and all of those apple martinis to get me in my partying mood ☺ Love you, my sistas!

Special thanks, again, to Bonnie McDuffie for helping me with the last-minute downloading projects. I appreciate all of your help!

Special thanks to Gardenia Parham (my partner in crime) for always being supportive of me and always taking time to listen to all of my venting. I love you girlfriend!

Thanks to my newfound family, the Fox's (Willie Fox Sr. (Granddad), Lenness Fox (Grandma),

Willie Fox Jr. (Dad), Victoria and Bernice). Since the day I've contacted you, you have shown me so much love. I am so happy to have you guys in my life. I love you all very much!

Thanks to my best friends, Daunise Kimball and Carl Hoffmann, for always being there for me and having a listening ear whenever I need one. I love you guys!

Thanks to my buddy, Darryl McNutt for being a great friend and taking the time out to have lunch with me from time to time! Oh, and thanks for keeping all of my secrets ☺

Thanks to Gary Norman (author of *Pink October*) for guiding me in publishing my book. I appreciate all of your help.

And a special thanks and shout-out to all of my other friends out there. You know who you are! ☺

PROLOGUE

I watched as they lowered the casket into the six-foot deep hole. My hands were shaking and my heart was broken. I hardly knew this woman, but the guilt wouldn't let me rest - I had to say my final goodbye and apologize to her yet once again. I remembered times when I wished this woman dead, but I didn't think it would happen – not this soon and not in that way. There was so much that I wanted to say. So many apologies I wanted to make, but now was too late. The tears wouldn't stop traveling down my caramel colored cheeks which were of a plum color when I left the house this morning, but the rainfall of tears washed all of the color away. I wanted to end the nightmares, clear my conscience and finally sleep again.

"Sophie was only 30 years old!" I thought to myself. "30 years old! Why did this have to happen? She didn't deserve this – no one deserves to die like this!" The more I thought of the situation, the angrier I became. I started to break down again. My whole body felt as if it were on fire and I felt that if I didn't hurry up and get out of there, I would faint and cause the family more grief than they already endured. Like they didn't have enough to worry about already!

An older woman, who looked exactly like Sophie, only older, comforted me. "You two were close?" she asked.

I didn't know how to respond to that question. Yes, I've had several encounters with Sophie, but there wasn't anything friendly about them. "Uh...yes, we were friends," I lied. And the lie only made me angrier with myself. "Are you her mother?" I asked trying to change the subject.

"Yes, baby," said Sophie's mother. "Sophie was my youngest baby. I can't believe she's gone. It's just not fair that a child goes before her parents. But it was her time. That's the way the Lord planned it - probably not in the way she went, but He planned for her to be with Him."

Sophie's mother tried her best to comfort me, but the more she spoke of her daughter, the angrier she became also.

"Oh, my sweet baby!" she cried. "My baby! My baby! My baby!"

I embraced Sophie's mother. At that moment, I wished it were me lying six feet deep. "I'm so sorry, Ms....."

"Just call me Paulette, everyone calls me that," Paulette said as she wiped the tears from her eyes.

"And you can call me Rita," I said. I tried my best to give Paulette a comforting smile, but that only made her stare harder at me. I was starting to feel very uncomfortable and more guilty than ever before.

"You look very familiar. Have we met before?" Paulette asked.

"I think I may have seen you around at my poetry club," I said as I looked away. I prayed that she wouldn't remember the evening of our encounter – the evening that I started to hate her daughter.

"Yes, of course. Soul Expressions, is it?" she asked.

I noticed that Paulette's voice was not as sweet as it was a second before.

"Yes, I am the owner," I said while feeling very uncomfortable.

"I've visited that place a couple of times. I always have a good time when I visit. That's where my baby met that…." Paulette went into a trance for a second and jumped out of it when I touched her arm. She never completed the rest of her sentence, but instead gave me another warm smile. "Well, thank you, baby. Thank you for being her friend. I can tell that you loved her very much."

That statement only made things worse. Why did she have to say that? I didn't love Sophie and Sophie didn't love me! I had lots of nerve for even showing up here! I had to get away. If I didn't get out of there, I was going to puke all over myself. I panicked. I grabbed Paulette's hand and rushed my goodbye. "Nice meeting you, Paulette. I gotta get out of here!…I mean…I have to leave.

I'm very sorry for your loss." My hands were trembling again and beads of sweat were starting to form on my forehead.

"Are you alright, baby?" she asked.

"I just gotta get out of here!" I screamed as I ran to my car. I didn't mean to be so dramatic, but I couldn't breathe. I felt as if the guilt was smothering me. I took several breaths trying to calm down. Nothing would rid me of my heartache. After I got in my Land Rover, locked the doors and rolled up my windows, I could no longer hold it all in. I scared myself by the way I was carrying on - like I was losing my mind! I decided to let it all out once and for all and that's when I screamed and beat the shit out of my dashboard. "I'm so sorry, Sophie! I'm so sorry!" I cried. "Please, please forgive me!"

* * * *

Chapter 1

Rita

I decided on a short, black, suede skirt to show off my beautifully toned legs, which also went perfect with my black leather vest, to wear on my blind date. It was freezing outside, but I was going for the *sexy* look. Black was definitely my color. It made my 150 pound frame slimmer, my long jet-black hair even darker and brought out a wild side in me that I never knew existed. Since my last breakup, I've been a little lonely so I decided to try Internet dating since I was so sick and tired of meeting no good men in nightclubs. And not just no good, I'm talking about toothless, receding hairline, married with 10 kids or men with money, but no common sense. So when I logged on to *singleblackworld.com*, I was hooked. There were over 100,000 selections of men on that site. But I wasn't going to be the fisherman, I wanted to be the bait. I felt that if God was going to send me someone, then that perfect man would have to come to me and I wouldn't have to go looking for him. But to give God a head start on finding my future husband, I downloaded my picture into the web site and created a personal profile...

> *Single Black Female Seeking Mature Male... Description of Myself: 35 years old, 150 pounds, Caramel Complexion, Long Black Hair, Dark Brown Eyes, Full Lips ...in other words, Beautiful. Looking for a man who can put a smile on my face; someone who enjoys getting out and enjoying life; long walks, dining, theatre, museums, etc. etc. etc. Also looking for someone who isn't afraid of new adventures. And most important, must be independent. If you are that special someone, please feel free to leave a note...*

The response was overwhelming! Fifty men responded to my page in less than 2 days. I guess that picture of myself from eight years ago worked – you know, the one I took when I was 20 pounds lighter! I've spoken with at least 10 of the men by e-mail, but decided that only one peaked my interest. His name was Brian and he would be my first date from cyberspace. He resembled that cute guy from the movie, "The Best Man" - you know, the man who went by the name of Quinton; at least that was what his picture showed him to look like. But, in other words, he was fine! He described himself as a 36 year-old, 6'3, 210 pound, outgoing and spontaneous construction company owner. Perfect for me! I've always wanted a man who complemented me and not just physically. He would have to be on my level financially, as well. I worked two jobs to put myself through college and after eight years of working as a paralegal, I finally saved enough money to start my own business. My poetry club, *Soul Expressions*, was the hottest in town.

The sound of the doorbell snapped me out of my daydream of finding the perfect man. I held my breath as I opened the door, hoping that this man looked liked the gorgeous man on the picture and not a Mr. Peabody look-a-like. "Well, hello!" I said as I laid my eyes on the most handsome man ever. It was him! It was the Quinton look-a-like!

"Hello, beautiful. I hope you are Rita," he said.

Was I tripping, or did his voice resemble that of the sexy after-hours V-103 talk show host? You know the one with the Barry White tone, with a hint of Denzel's smoothness. Okay, I was tripping. While his voice was not even close to Barry's, he definitely was a "Quinton-look-a-like".

Hell, I don't even think Quinton looked this damn good in person. "That would be me," I said. I noticed a quiver in my voice. Damn, I was nervous!

"You're even more beautiful in person, Rita," he said.

I blushed. "You're not so bad yourself. Would you like to come in for a drink before we head out?"

Brian walked in with a confident stride. He noticed from the way I looked at him, that if he continued to use his charm, I would be all his.

"Yes, thank you. What do you have?" he asked.

"What do you mean?"

"What do you have to drink?"

"Oh. I'm sorry," I said feeling dumber than a 5 year old in a college classroom. "Is red wine okay?" I asked nervously.

"Red wine will be fine. You have a nice place here," he said.

"Thank you", I said as I handed Brian his drink and directed him to my sofa. Let's sit down for a few minutes and get to know each other a little better before we head out."

"Okay. I'll start," he said.

Who did he think he was volunteering himself to go first? Now that was a turn off and I was ready to call off the date, but changed my mind due to the fact that he was so damn gorgeous. After that, I prayed that this man didn't have an ego the size of Mount Rushmore. But, hell, who could blame him? He'd probably had so many women stepping to him that he'd heard it all already.

His conversation was a little boring at first, but I didn't care. I wanted to slap myself for my weakness. He was doing most of the talking, and I couldn't concentrate on anything that came out of his mouth. His appearance had my mind going in a million different directions: *Brian is fine, but he's still a man so be careful – but damn, look at those eyes - are those hazel eyes really his? Oh my, look at his teeth - I've never seen teeth that straight! Is that a Versace jacket? He must have a little money. Okay, girl! Get it together!*

Brian noticed that I ignored his every word. "Are you okay, Rita?" he asked as he gave me his *"I'm too sexy"* smile.

"I'm so sorry, Brian. I'm just a little nervous. I....."

"Don't worry about it. Are you ready to go?"

"I guess so."

I was pissed at myself. I acted as if I've never had someone so fucking handsome in my face before. I felt like such a damn fool. Such a stupid fucking fool! I had to put it in my head that I was not in fucking high school and I needed to start acting like I had some fucking sense. Did I mention that I used the "f" word a lot when I got nervous?

I forgave myself for playing the dense woman role and pulled myself together. I grabbed his hand, looked into his eyes, and told my future baby's daddy: "Let's go and make this a magical evening."

* * * *

Brian pulled up in front of the *Piper's Den*, which was considered as one of the cheapest restaurants in town. I was very disappointed. Okay, I was pissed! Not only in his choice of restaurant and the lack of conversation on the way to the cheap restaurant, but also in the 82' Ford Pinto with the rust on the hood that he chose to drive me around in. At every red light, I had to pretend to look down in my purse so that no one would see my face. Not only was the car ugly, but it was loud as hell. And on top of all of this, he acted as if he wasn't bothered or embarrassed to drive me around in it because he just kept going on and on about how good I looked in my vest. *"That's okay girl, you can change him...Make him into the man that you want him to be,"* I had to keep repeating to myself. Thank God we were there. I hopped out of the raggedly bucket before he could come around and open the door for me.

Brian noticed the expression on my face when I got out of the car. "Look, I'm sorry about the car," he said. "My truck is in the shop and this old thing is the only car I have right now. I've had it since I was 16. It's like my baby."

"Oh, it's no problem," I lied. *"Time to give the baby up for adoption,"* I thought. I put on a phony smile and grabbed Brian's hand. We walked into the restaurant, hand in hand, looking like the perfect couple. All eyes were on us as the waitress with the gold hair, gold earrings and gold lipstick led us to our table.

"What can I get yall to drank?" the waitress asked.

"I'll start with a glass of water," I said. I didn't care for anything on the menu. I couldn't believe that he chose such a low-class place to take me on our first date. I had to keep telling myself to give him a chance. I would be a fool not to give him a try. Brian was the type of man that I could show off to all of my patrons and friends.

"I'll have a Heineken," Brian said while eyeing the menu.

The waitress popped her bubble gum. "Okay, I'll be back for yall's food order." She walked away, popping her bubble gum even louder.

"Ever been here?" Brian asked.

"No," I said. I wanted to scream *"Hell No!"* "What's good here?"

"Oh, man! They got the best chicken wing dinner! It comes with four barbecue wings, fries and a drink. I want you to try it."

"Chicken Wings! I want a steak! Bake Potato! Salad! Anything but chicken wings!" I screamed to myself. I looked at Brian's cheap, fine ass and gave him my biggest smile. "Yummy! I guess I'll have to try it, then."

The waitress returned to take our wing dinner order. I wanted and needed to know more about Brian. So far, this date was not going so well. "So, what is it that you do again....for a living?" I asked, trying not to sound too serious about the question.

"I'm a construction worker."

A fly must have buzzed by my ears because I was sure that I didn't hear him right. "You mean you're a construction company owner, right?"

"Well....er....um...no. I just put that on the website. I am, however, an employee of Herron Construction Co. I hope you're not disappointed. I wanted to meet you so badly that I changed my profile around a little before I responded to your page. I figured you wouldn't have accepted this date, unless I was some sort of entrepreneur."

I was furious but decided not to show my anger. Usually, that would have been my cue to call a taxi and get my ass out of there, but I just had to have this man wealthy or not. "Why would you think that?" I said with a chuckle trying to convince myself that it was no big deal. "I stated that I wanted an independent man, not necessarily rich, but one who could take care of himself." I thought it was kind of cute how he tricked me into our date, but on the same note, he lied. There was no way in hell that I would have accepted this date if he had not put down that he owned the damn company. One of my main pet peeves was that I couldn't stand a broke ass man. But on the other hand, I was glad I accepted the date. He was too fine for words; besides, he did have a job, didn't he?

"What is it that you do?" he asked.

"I own the *Soul Expressions* poetry club here in the city," I said proudly.

"Really?"

"Yes. You should drop by some time. Friday nights is our poetry slam. We have famous poets stop by all the time. As a matter of fact, our special guest this Friday is LadySeas. She's a hot new poet here in Chicago."

"So, are you saying you want to see me again?"

I blushed. Something came over me. I grabbed his hand and looked into his pretty eyes and gave him my *"you aint going nowhere"* smile. "Of course, I do. I hope you feel the same."

"Damn skippy, I feel the same," he said. "I think you and I will have a good time together."

I blushed.

The waitress, after about 40 minutes, brought the food to our table. The chicken wings were either delicious or I was starving. I didn't bother to drink any of my water for the stains on the glass grossed me the hell out. Me and Brian flirted the rest of the night. Halfway through dinner, Brian noticed that I spilled a little barbecue sauce on my vest, right between my breasts. He took his napkin and wiped it off, slowly. The more he wiped, the hotter I became. If we weren't in cheaprestaurantville, I would have taken my clothes off right then and there and gave him a little something something for dessert.

"So, Ms. Rita, what are your plans for the rest of the evening?" he asked seductively.

"I don't know," I said. "We'll just have to see where the night leads us."

The night did indeed lead us - straight to my downtown tri-level townhouse. I couldn't believe I was getting ready to sleep with him on the first date for that was just not my style. But something about Brian brought out the nasty girl in me. I was hotter than a Popeye's pepper. I barely got the keys in the door when Brian started to plant feather kisses on the back of my neck. "Ooooh...yeah...damn...that's my spot," I moaned. It had been a while since I got me some good stuff, but I didn't want him to know that. I wanted to seem like I knew what I was doing - a pro, but not quite a hoe. I led Brian to the couch, and Brian, in turn, pulled me into his arms. He kissed me so affectionately that I started to feel so comfortable with him – like I've known him for more than just 5 hours. I pulled away from the kiss, afraid that I would fall in love if I continued it. I cursed myself for being weak that way. I had to get away from the kiss so I stood up and started to dance seductively. My friend, Jackie, once told me: *"girl, a man loves when you dance for him... dance for him one time and he's like putty in your hands... dance for him and you can get a brother to do anything you want."* That's exactly what I was trying to achieve. I wanted Brian to be putty in my arms; to do any and everything to my body that I desired. During the strip tease, I removed my clothing as I looked into his catty eyes. Brian then removed his clothing and started to kiss me from my forehead down to my feet. I moaned with pleasure. Brian took his time with me. He lowered his body so that his face was directly in front of my love triangle and commenced to eating me like I was the steak dinner I thought I would have earlier that night.

"Oooooh....ooooooh...OOOOOH!" I moaned. His tongue felt so good down there, but I wanted him to slow down; I didn't want the wonderful pleasure to end so soon. But Brian worked his tongue like a professional, and before I knew it, my eyes popped open and I felt like I exploded into a million pieces. "OOOOOH...ooooooh.....Yes!...oh, baby, Yes!" I screamed. It had been a while since any man made me cum like that. I was very satisfied. Brian then stood revealing a cute little smirk on his face. I guess that was my cue to return the favor – but there was one problem – I refused to put this man's penis in my mouth on the first date. To play it off, I advised Brian to lay down on the couch. I then kissed him softly and slowly on his neck, down to his chest and then his navel, but I stopped there. I went up to his face and gave him another passionate kiss on the mouth as I put a condom on his nicely curved penis. He tried to stop me for he wanted me to perform the same thing that he just did for me. But before he could say anything, I positioned myself on top of him and started to ride him like a champ.

Brian was impressed. *"Who needed a blow job when a sister can ride you like this!"* he thought to himself as he reached his much-anticipated climax.

Brian's facial expression told all, although he didn't make a sound. He was enjoying my riding technique. When he finally came, he made the ugliest face I'd ever seen come from a fine ass man, but that didn't bother me. I knew what he looked like when his face wasn't all scrunched up. We held each other for a moment when Brian started to mumble something about how lucky he was to find me. I stared at him as he drifted off to sleep. *"Damn, I must have really put it on him if he's asleep already!"* I commended myself on such a good job, covered Brian with a blanket and headed upstairs to shower and get a good night's rest. I didn't want to awaken him for he looked so cute laying on my couch. I could see him laying there every night, or, better yet, in my bed every night. "Good night, Brian," I whispered as I headed towards my spiral staircase to climb onto my other man – my mattress.

* * * *

Chapter 2
Sophie

"Get the hell out of here, you cheating bastard!" Sophie screamed. "And get the hell out of my closet, you trifling bitch!"

The younger, petite and very scared woman exited the closet.

"I didn't know he was married! Please, don't hurt me!" the woman pleaded.

"Just get the fuck out of my house!" Sophie screamed. The woman ran out faster than a coyote.

Sophie's husband, Ahmad, was also afraid. He knew Sophie had a bad temper and when she got mad, he'd better watch out. "Baby, what are you doing home so early? I....I....I thought you said you were working late," he said while standing butt naked in front of their bedroom window.

"That's what I told you! I knew something wasn't right when I left this morning! Did you think that I couldn't hear your telephone conversation you were trying to be so discreet about this morning! Who do you think I am…some sort of dumb woman or something? Sophie was fuming. She looked around for the biggest piece of anything so that she could knock her husband's head off.

Ahmad was even more afraid now that he saw his wife was about to get violent. He tried to run past her. Sophie grabbed him by his balls. "Awwwwwwwwwwww!" he screamed. "Let me go, Sophie! Please! Awwwwwwwwww!"

"I'll let you go, but you'd better promise me one thing before I do!"

"Anything! Awwwwwwwwww!" Ahmad was in so much pain that he promised himself right then and there that cheating was no longer his thing.

"When I file for my divorce, which I will do first thing tomorrow morning, I don't want any problems out of you. I want the money, all of it. I want the house and I want the cars. If I don't get what I want out of this divorce, then you'd better watch your back. Do you understand?"

"Yes….awwwww…yes. I understand."

Sophie let him go. He dropped to the floor like he wanted to say a prayer of "thanks".

"Baby, please don't divorce me....I'm so sorry...I love you....I didn't mean.....," he begged.

Sophie bent down to grab his balls again. He jumped up and ran away from her all while protecting his balls with both of his hands. "Okay, okay! I'll move my stuff out today!"

"Yes, you will move out today. And leave the keys on the fireplace mantle by the front door. The next time I see you, it will be in court. By the way, I don't care how sorry you are. I've been knowing about your affairs since day one and I tried to pretend that I didn't care. But now you have taken it too far with bringing the hoochies home and screwing them in our bed. You were a worthless piece of shit when I met you and you still are. Get the hell out of my house. You have exactly 30 minutes to pack and get out. Or else!"

"Okay, Sophie. If that's the way you want it."

"You're damn right, that's the way I want it!"

Sophie walked to her 4-car garage. She looked down at her watch. "28 minutes!" she yelled. As brave as she tried to be in this situation, she actually wanted to cry her heart out. *"Why did that bastard do this to me? What is wrong with me? I'm a beautiful woman! What did I do to deserve this?"* All sorts of thoughts crossed her mind. She opened up the door to her brand new Benz and got in. She looked down at her watch again. *"20 minutes..."* A tear dared to come out from under her lid. *"No, no, no, girlfriend. Don't you dare cry over that man."* And with that thought, the tears stopped. Sophie vowed after her last relationship that she would not shed one more tear over any man. It seemed as if every one of her relationships ended because of another woman who couldn't find her own man. She looked down at her watch once more.

At that moment, Ahmad entered the garage to load the trunk with his suitcases. He paused when he saw Sophie. He wanted to hold her and promise her whatever she wanted if only she'd forgive him and take him back. He really loved her, he was just not a one-woman type of man. The look Sophie gave him reminded him that he'd better not even dare to say one word. Without any goodbyes, Ahmad got in his car and drove off.

And no matter how hard she tried not to, Sophie couldn't help it, she cried.

* * * *

Chapter 3
Brian

Brian usually didn't meet women online, but he started to develop a bad reputation around town, thanks to his ex-girlfriends' big mouths. He saw that Rita was new to online dating and when he pulled up her picture, he didn't recognize her from any of the clubs he hung around. And by the way she looked last night in her short skirt and that vest that made her breasts look like two perfectly round oranges, he figured that she craved attention. *"This is going to be too easy,"* he thought to himself. From past experiences, he knew why Rita couldn't concentrate when she was around him. His looks were his weapon. He could look a woman in her eyes and she would be hypnotized, just like that. He thanked his parents everyday for blessing him with the looks of a god.

He was still full from the breakfast Rita prepared for him this morning, and drained from the passionate sex that went down after breakfast. Brian smiled to himself as he thought of how hooked this woman was on him after only one date. He crept into his mother's house, careful not to run into her.

"Uh huh! I see you trying to sneak yo' butt in my house! Where you been? Out with one of them hussies again?" Faye asked her son.

"Damn, ma! Why are you always sneaking to wait up for me?" Brian couldn't wait to move from his mother's house. He had been there for over three month's now after his ex-finance' kicked him out of her house and ended the engagement.

"What do you mean, waiting up? Boy, this is my house! I aint got to sneak around my own house just cus' you here! Now where have you been? You know you was spose' to go job hunting this morning!"

"I know, ma…..I just forgot, that's all. It's so hard trying to find work in the construction field, especially since the season hasn't started yet."

"Boy! You are 30 years old now. It's time for you to get your shit together! I'm tired of you always trying to live up under some woman or back here with me. I don't know why they take care of your lazy behind. I'm yo' momma so I don't mind every now and then, but you getting way too old now. Me and your daddy raised you better than that!"

Brian knew his mother was upset so he let her have the last word. Every time his mother mentioned his father, he knew not to continue the conversation. She missed him and so did he. He kissed his mother on the cheek and headed towards his bedroom.

Faye disappointedly shook her head. She loved her son dearly, but was starting to get disgusted with him. He was becoming a carbon copy of his father, only he didn't know it. Faye made sure that Brian never heard one argument between her and his father. If he had, he would know about the other women and the occasional fights between them. She knew about Brian's obsession with women and how he treated them and it surprised her. Now how is it that he turned out to be exactly like his father? She remembered times when she begged her son to seek counseling for his problem, but as usual, Brian ignored her. She decided to keep quiet on the matter. There was no sense in repeating the same thing to him over and over again. It will take him to mess with the wrong woman to get him straightened out. Ever since his father passed last year, Brian has tried, but failed, to clean up his act. *"Treat the ladies like queens, son"* were the last words Brian would hear from his father. Faye wished that her husband would have followed his own advice. Faye then remembered the clutter Brian left earlier in his bedroom. "Clean up that room, Brian! It's a mess!" she screamed.

Brian giggled. She always made him feel like he was 18 again. Oh, how he'd wished to be 18 again. That was when he really got everything he wanted – jewelry, clothing and money. The women spoiled him so. He remembered dating 11 women at one time who all lived in the same town. He was so smooth with his game that he never got caught. He also made sure to keep a diary on each woman so he wouldn't get confused as to who said what, when, how or where. Brian never quite had any male friends, but that didn't bother him. He referred to them all as "playa haters". But he was getting older now. He could only handle one, maybe two at a time these days. He figured either the women were getting smarter or he was losing his touch.

Faye went up to her son's bedroom and knocked on the door.

"Come in, ma."

Faye was shocked to see her son cleaning his room. He rarely put a smile on her face these days, but seeing him clean his room actually pleased her. "Brian, Leona called again," she said.

"What did she want?" he asked as he felt his body tense up. He hated hearing his ex-fiancé's name. Leona was the first woman that Brian ever fell in love with. He wanted to marry her and finally settle down to please his father, but everything turned sour in the relationship. After his breakup with Leona, Brian swore that he would never let his heart get in the way of his relationships ever again.

"She said she'd drop the charges on one condition."

Brian hated hearing these messages coming from his mother. That was one of the reasons why he lost a little respect for Leona and treated her the way he did. She tried to turn his mother against him by always telling his every move. No wonder his mother looks at him totally different now. He used to be her *"baby"* and now, he's just *"Brian"*. "What condition?"

"I don't know. You have to call her yourself. Believe it or not, she wouldn't tell me," Faye said as she walked back to the kitchen to chug down the rest of her Colt 45.

"Now, that, I can't believe. She usually tells you everything else," he mumbled. Brian grabbed the telephone on the dresser next to his king size bed. As he dialed Leona's number, he noticed how nervous he was. He didn't want to go back to jail. He was too damn pretty for jail.

He didn't mean to hit Leona as hard as he did the last time they were together, but she pressed charges anyway. And that pissed him off. After he was released on an I-bond, he charged up to the hospital to give her a piece of his mind. He'd remembered that day as if it were yesterday. But after seeing Leona with two black eyes, a swollen lip, a broken arm and a broken leg, he realized that he deserved those 10 hours behind bars. He apologized to her several times when he saw her, forcing the tears to come to his eyes. "I'm so sorry, baby. I didn't mean to hurt you like this," he cried. Leona was tired of his apologies and told him to get his shit and get the hell out of her house before she was released from the hospital. Brian still has not gotten over her and wishes that he never fell in love with her in the first place.

Leona answered the phone on the second ring. "Hello."

"Leona, this is Brian. What's up?"

"Look, Brian, I didn't leave that message with your mom so that we can be all chummy. I want this to be the very last telephone call between us."

"Damn, are you still mad at me?"

"I'll always be mad at you, Brian. I hate you!"

"Whatever. You don't have to be like that. I told you I was sorry. Well, anyway, what is this condition you're giving me?"

"The condition is that I never see you around my house or job again. I don't even want to see you at the gas station up the street…just stay the hell away from me!"

"Damn, it's like that?" he asked.

Leona's voice trembled. "You don't think I recognized your raggedly ass car across the street from my job last week? Are you stalking me?"

"Hell no, I'm not stalking you! I was just in the neighborhood and wanted to talk to you, but you ran off so fast."

"Well, I need you to stop coming around. That scares me. I'm tired of always having to look over my shoulders. I don't trust you anymore.

Brian couldn't believe that she felt that way. "What are you thinking? You think I'm crazy or something? That I would hurt you?"

"Brian, I'm still recovering from our last incident.... Look, I don't want to talk about it! Please! Now, if you want the charges dropped, that's all I want you to do, okay?"

"Are you dating someone else already?"

"None of your damn business, Brian!"

"Baby, I still love you. Why are you acting like this?" Brian asked almost desperately.

"Brian, either stay the hell away from me, or else spend the next 5 to 10 years in jail."

"Well, since you put it that way, it's a deal. You don't ever have to worry about seeing me again!"

"Fine. I'll drop the charges then. And if I do see that you violated our agreement, then believe me, I'll get the case reopened," Leona said before she hung up.

Brian was excited about not having to worry about being charged, but was also hurt by the agreement. "Damn!" was all he could say. He sucked it all in and exhaled. "Well, life goes on," he said to himself. He picked up the telephone and dialed Rita's number. The call went straight to Rita's answering machine. *Hi, this is Rita, I'm not home right now, so please leave a message and I'll call you as soon as I can. Beep!* "Hey, Rita. This is Brian. Just wanted to thank you again for that wonderful night and even better morning. I'm headed out to find work...I mean, I'm headed out to work right now, but please, when you get a chance, call me. You've been on my mind all day. Baby, I think I'm seriously falling for you. Bye, now!"

A devilish grin crossed his face. "Now that's a message of a true playa playa."

* * * *

Chapter 4

Brian had me hooked. I couldn't get him out of my mind. It had been a while since I felt this way about anyone. I tried to concentrate on satisfying my customers and poets. *Soul Expressions* was packed. There were several poets on the roster for the evening and it looked to be a long night. I didn't expect my club to be as crowded as it was on a Tuesday night, but with the way things were going with Brian, the success of the club didn't surprise me. Everything in my life was finally going great. I figured it was my time to shine, especially after all the bad luck I had in the past.

It had been a week since I'd last seen Brian and I was feigning for him. I couldn't wait to touch him again, especially after our daily conversations and the several sweet voicemails he'd left me. He had been trying to come over to my house every night, but my schedule wouldn't allow me to meet with him. I was dead tired by the time I left the club and it was just entirely too late for me to have company – I didn't want Brian to feel like he was my booty call. I pleaded for him to come by the club, but he claimed his work schedule wouldn't permit him to get away. Our schedules always clashed. I did notice how Brian changed the subject every time I mentioned my coming by his job to take him to lunch since I was almost always available in the afternoons. He finally agreed that he would stop by the club on Friday evening. I couldn't wait.

It was time to get the show started. I stepped on stage to introduce the first poet of the evening. "And now, ladies and gentlemen, here's one of our regulars coming to the mike. Please give a warm welcome for Shyfox!" The crowd went wild. Shyfox always worked the room with her pieces and was one of the few poets who didn't confuse you with her words. Her poems were straight to the point. Shyfox grabbed the mike and, with feeling and power in her voice, recited her famous piece, *"Baby Momma Drama"*:

How is it "drama" when you're always in hiding
When she's crying for you, I'm the one by her side
When the birthdays came by, you aint never around
You always have a reason for letting her down
How is it drama, my brotha? When all I ask for is help
You act like you don't love her, that you just care for yourself!
When I yell at you for not doing your part
You say I'm always talking shit - And that you didn't want kids from the start
You think I was ready, my nucca? guess what - I wasn't
I told you to pull out when you said "baby, I'm cumming"
So here we are with this beautiful little girl
And I wouldn't give her back for nuthin' in this world

Apology From One Sista' To Another

And all I ask from you is that you show her you care
And when she cries for her "daddy" that you will be there
I don't give two shits that you don't want to be with me
I just know how it is to be raised without a daddy
I never had a male role model in my life
I saw what my mom went through night after night
So you keep hollering that it's drama, but you'll reap what you sow
She'll grow up and forget about you and wouldn't know you from Joe...
And then as soon as your immature ass grows up and want to be a father
She'll dodge you and curse you cuz you didn't even bother...
To help her mom to pay for her education
And medical bills, food, clothes, shelter and other situations
And she'll think back to when her birthday and X-mas came around
That you didn't bother to send her a gift, call her - And how it always brought her down
Baby momma drama is just a lame term...
There's a reason I'm mad at you, When will you learn?
When I asks you for cash, just give me what I need
And remember that I'm the mother of your beautiful seed
And when I ask you to watch her from time to time
It's only cuz I need a break - is that a crime?
It's not fair that we both made this child
And I'm the one always at home - and you're out there running wild!
What we need to do is talk about a plan, so come by and holla
Then you won't have to worry about no "baby momma drama"!

As usual, Shyfox received a standing ovation, especially from the single mothers in the room. You could tell by the way some of the men were clapping with a frown, that they were the dead beats. I walked toward the stage to hug Shyfox and to commend her on such a great job, but on my way to the stage, I saw a familiar face. It was Brian and he was looking better than the first time I'd seen him. There was something about a man dressed in thug gear. It was sexy. His six feet, 3 inch fine self was sporting a pair of Tommy jeans which were not too tight and not too big; they were a perfect fit, and thankfully, not sagging in the least bit. He wore a crisp white T-shirt with a Tommy logo which showed off his well-defined arms and on top of his head was a blue Tommy baseball cap. I was totally turned on. Don't get me wrong, there isn't anything wrong with a brother in a suit, but there is just something about a man in jeans and T-shirt that melts my butter. I signaled for my manager to introduce the next poet. I then signaled for Brian to follow me into the back of the club, which was my office.

"Hey! What are you doing here? I thought you said you would stop by on Friday?" I said with a huge grin on my face. I was too happy to see him.

"I wanted to surprise you with these," he said as he pulled out a bouquet of roses. "Besides, I couldn't wait that long to see you."

"You are so sweet." I sniffed the beautiful flowers and felt like a rose myself. I felt pretty and layered. Now when I say layered, I mean that now that I was with Brian again, I was so hot, and I felt like I wanted to remove all of the layers of clothing I had on. Brian's stare-me-down was starting to make me uncomfortable so I went to my desk to pull out a vase to fill with water and place my lovely bouquet. "So, how do you like the club so far?" I asked.

"Shyfox put a chill through my body with that piece. I'm glad I don't have any shorties," he lied.

"I know. She did a fantastic job." I was so nervous when I was around this man. I didn't know if that was a good or bad thing. Something about him made me feel weak in the knees. I was starting to feel nauseous. "Um...so....you want to go back out there?" I asked.

"No. I want to stay in here with you." He kissed me on the forehead and looked into my eyes.

I couldn't help it – I looked away.

"What's wrong, baby?" he asked.

"Brian, I don't know exactly what I'm doing. I really like you. I just want to make sure that we're both on the same level of things here."

"Gotcha!" he thought. "Rita, I can't get you out of my head. I don't know what this feeling is, but I know it's a feeling that I don't mind having. Can we make this official? Will you be my lady?"

I was surprised by his question. I had only been out with him once. He took my statement to a whole new level. When I mentioned being on the same level, I didn't mean having a girlfriend/boyfriend relationship. I was speaking of slowing things down a little for I was still embarrassed for sleeping with him on our first date. The way he asked me seemed kind of cute though, almost elementary-like. I smiled nervously and decided to take advantage of the moment. "You mean, me and you, one-on-one, exclusive?"

"That's exactly what I mean," he said. "I'm getting too old to be playing the field. You are exactly what I'm looking for in a woman and, stop me if you think I'm going too far when I tell you this....but....I think I'm falling in love with you."

My mouth hung open and my mind went wild. *Did he just say he loved me? No, he said he's in love with me! Isn't that the same thing?*

"Rita!" Brian broke me out of my trance.

"Oh. I'm sorry. I'm just shocked by the suddenness of everything. I...I....think I'm in love with you too.....um......are you sure you know me well enough for a relationship?" I could not believe how fast this brother moved and I wasn't mad at him – not mad at all.

"The day I pulled your picture up on *singleblackworld.com* is the day I knew I wanted to be with you." Brian gave himself a few playa points for coming up with that line. He loved the way the words flowed out of his mouth so naturally.

"Oh, how sweet, Brian," I blushed. *How did I get so lucky? Here is a man – no, a fine, working and sweet man – asking me to be his woman. Don't you pass up this opportunity, Rita – you can get to know him later. How can I say no?* I grabbed Brian's hand and planted a kiss in his palm. "Yes, Brian. I will be your lady."

Brian grinned. "Well, honey, let's show the world that we're a couple. He grabbed my hand and led me out to the club.

I felt like the First Lady of the United States with my fine ass president on my arms as I walked, or more like floated, into the main hall of the poetry club. A few of the patrons smiled my way. Some of my regulars, mainly women and surprisingly a few men, gave me the thumbs up as I flaunted my gorgeous new boyfriend.

* * * *

Chapter 5

Sophie sat out on her deck, a glass of champagne in hand, reminiscing of when her and Ahmad first purchased their 4-story Victorian home. That was the second happiest day in her life, her wedding, the first.

Sophie knew all along that her husband was screwing around on her, even on the morning of her wedding day, but she kept quiet about it. Ahmad was wealthy and she didn't want to do anything to jeopardize her stable future.

It wasn't as if her husband didn't love her. Even with all of his mistresses, he still loved her. Ahmad's cheating was fine with Sophie - having another woman in her very own bed was what caused the divorce. So long as Ahmad never flaunted his affairs in her face, she would have kept going along with the marriage. As far as she was concerned, he totally disrespected her by laying up with another woman on her $25,000 bed – her treasure. The nerve!

She didn't realize that she would hurt as much after finalizing their divorce; however, she still had a stable future, thanks to the two-timing bastard. Ahmad signed every legal document granting her the house, two cars - the Benz and the Jaguar and enough money to last a lifetime. She was surprised that her little threat scared the shit out of him for she was just a little woman with a big mouth. By Ahmad being the CEO of AMS Consulting Corporation and the way he bossed his employees around, everyone assumed that he had a hold on Sophie. If only they knew the truth; Ahmad was a big baby behind closed doors. Ahmad must have thought she was a crazy bitch by the way she grabbed his balls. She laughed at the thought. Or maybe the guilt of how their marriage ended made Ahmad feel that that was the least he could do after all the years of infidelity.

Sophie walked into her big and lonely house. She sulked in depression. *What will I do now? No man, no children.* Sophie found her stash. She hadn't rolled a joint in so long, but was surprised to see that she still had that touch; her joint was rolled perfectly. Her marijuana was the only source she could rely on these days to ease her mind. Ahmad discovered later on in their marriage that Sophie had a really bad habit with it. He convinced her to quit - said it wasn't lady-like. But Ahmad wasn't here now. Sophie took a pull of her weed and, instantly, she felt the effects. She continued to smoke it until she had no feeling - no emotion.

She felt like singing so she played Anita Baker's *"Giving You The Best That I Got"*. She swirled around her luxurious living room while singing. *I'll tell you now that I've made a vow, I'm giving you the best that I got, babeeeeeee. I'll bet everything on my wedding ring...*. This song reminded her of Ahmad. Whenever he pissed her off, she made sure to play this song. Ahmad would feel so guilty that he would go out and buy her the latest jewelry from Tiffany's. Boy, she could really use some new jewelry right about now. She programmed her cd player to repeat this song and she sang the hell out of it until her high went down. She hated that she was starting to get sober again; she wasn't ready to go back to reality, but she also promised herself not to go back to her 5-joint-a-day habit either.

Sophie always instantly became hungry after smoking a joint. She went into the kitchen and made herself a huge turkey sandwich. She then walked into her bedroom and fell out onto the bed. As soon as her head hit the pillow, she was out for the count.

* * *

Chapter 6

Sophie realized that money couldn't supply happiness. Five months have passed and she'd only stepped out of her house to retrieve the morning paper. She was still depressed and the marijuana no longer made her happy. She started to pick up weight with all of the eating caused by the marijuana which made her hungrier than an alley cat. The depression went to an all-time low when she found out that Ahmad married one of his mistresses. Not only that, but had nerve to have a load of money stashed away in an out-of-country bank account. Now she knew why he signed the divorce papers so fast. She didn't have the strength to pursue a lawsuit against him. Besides, she had more than enough money.

The telephone frightened her. Since the divorce, she rarely received telephone calls. Her friends were actually the wives of Ahmad's friends and when he left, so did they. It could only be one person, her mother, who called her every day around this time.

Sophie perked up before answering the telephone. "Hello."

"Hey baby!" Paulette screamed. Whitney Houston's, *"I'm Every Woman,"* blasted in the background.

"Mother, please turn that music down before you give me a headache!"

"Hold on!"

Sophie prepared herself for the "*get up and move on with your life*" speech her mother gave every day since the divorce.

"Okay, I'm back. So, how's my baby today?"

"I'm fine, mother."

"You know what I was thinking, baby? I think that we need to go out. We haven't had a mother-daughter outing in a while," Paulette said.

"What! No speech today, mom?"

"I knew you were going to say that. Don't be a smarty pants. I was only saying that for your own good and since you're still laying up in that house, I figured I'll take the initiative and get you out of there."

"Well, thanks, ma. I really appreciate this." That was exactly what she needed – to get out and stop feeling sorry for herself. "Where do you want to go?"

"I heard great things about that new poetry club downtown. I think it's called *Soul Expressions* or something like that. Let's go and check it out tomorrow night. I heard they were having some sort of black tie party."

Did Sophie hear her mother correctly? Poetry? "Mother, what do *you* know about poetry?"

"Chile, I will have you know that I've read several poems. Some of my favorites are Nikki Giovanni, Saul Williams, Sonia Sanchez and Maya Angelou."

"Well, excuse me! I guess you do know your poetry. I'm not really into that sort of thing, but I would love to check out the club with you. See you tomorrow, ma. I love you."

"Love you too baby. See you tomorrow."

Sophie adored her mother. Paulette was the kind of mother who, no matter how tired she was, always made time for her children. If anyone could get her out of this funk, it was her mother.

Sophie had so much to do in so little time. She needed to get her hair done, a pedicure and manicure. After five months of not stepping in a beauty and nail salon, she knew she would have to tip generously. She dialed the salon's number while crossing her fingers. "Please, please have an opening" she prayed.

* * * *

Chapter 7

"Brian, I really need to be at the club tomorrow night. You know how busy Fridays are!" I was starting to get irritated with my new broke ass man.

"Can't you take an evening off?" Brian asked using his pretty boy charm. "Come on, let's go to Disneyland this weekend. Please!"

"And who's going to pay for it, Brian? Me? You never have a problem with spending my money. You're lucky I forgave you for lying to me about that damn construction job. You could have told me you got laid off up front!"

"Ah, come on, baby. Don't start that again. What's in the past is in the past. It's our five month anniversary this weekend. I just thought that we'd do something different for a change."

"Well your not working is not in the past. Let's talk about that!"

"Look!" Brian yelled. He was tired of having the same conversation with Rita. "I told you. No one will hire me right now. There is an overload of construction workers. I am on call with five companies! Give me a break, damn it!"

Brian never spoke to me in that tone before. I didn't realize that he was as frustrated as he was with his not working. Shame on me for throwing that in his face. "I'm sorry, baby. I didn't mean to upset you." I put my arms around my man and told him again how sorry I was.

Brian held in the crooked grin that was so anxious to cross his face. *"You are too easy,"* he thought.

I felt sorry for him. He'd finally confessed to not having a job within three weeks of our relationship after I asked him why he never wanted to take me out on a real date. He always wanted to come over to my place and chill out instead of getting out and spending money. It was only when I said "my treat" that he was willing to jump up and get excited about going out.

I was angry at first by all of his confessions, but he looked so pitiful when he confessed, I understood that it was hurting him as much as it hurts me.

I had no problem paying for our meals, but when he started to ask me to loan him money for clothing and jewelry that he just so had to have, I started to look at him differently. I would buy them for him though, to prevent an argument. Brian was such a big baby at times and I always gave in to his pleadings. It wasn't that big of a deal though; besides, I loved to see my man looking good.

After discovering the truth of Brian not having a truck "in the shop", I, not wanting to step another foot in the poisonous Pinto, surprised my man with a brand new Cadillac. If I was going to be seen with a man as fine as Brian, I was going to be seen riding in style.

Like I said earlier, it wasn't a big deal; however, I was starting to feel a tad bit used. Even after I tried to help him find a job by preparing his resume and faxing them out for him, when he got a call for an interview, he'd never show up. His excuse was that he wanted to try and start his own construction company and that he did not want to work for the *man* anymore. Now don't get me wrong, I didn't mind that he had huge goals, but how did he expect to start a construction company lying around on my damn sofa?

I knew deep down inside that I should let him go, but I was so whipped by his charm and by the way he made my body feel after a 3-hour love session. I know, that's no excuse. The total truth was that I didn't want to be alone again. Yes, I did break my own rule of not dating a "broke ass man", but I guess there was always a first time for everything.

One thing I never regretted was the fact that I invited Brian to move into my townhouse. Four months into the relationship, Brian started to complain about his mother being on his back about everything. Back in my early 20's, I lived with my mom, may she rest in peace, and knew exactly how it could be with living with parents so I kind of felt pity for him and told him he could stay at my house for a few days. Those few days turned out to be one month and counting. Despite his unemployment situation, I enjoyed coming home to my man. I felt like I was playing a grown-up game of house.

I knew that I spoiled him, but hell, I couldn't help it. I actually enjoyed putting a smile on my baby's face when I surprised him with expensive gifts.

I kissed Brian softly on his spot behind his ear and apologized again. "I'm sorry baby. I'll tell you what. Why don't you go to the club with me tomorrow night? I'll have a special bottle of champagne waiting on our table and will make the reservations for Florida first thing Saturday morning, which means that we would be dancing with Mickey by Saturday afternoon. Sound good?"

"Yeah, baby, that sounds real good," he said as he lifted me in his arms.

My baby was so strong and masculine. He carried me into the bedroom and gently lay me down and kissed me passionately.

"I love you," he said.

"Brian, do you mean that?" I blushed. That was the first time that he said those three sweet words to me.

"Yes, I do. I'm not going anywhere, baby. You are the best thing that has ever happened to me."

"Really?"

"Really."

"I am so in love with you, Brian," I said in a rushed manner as if I had been holding those words in for years. "I've never been happier with anyone else. I have a history of bad relationships, but whatever it takes, I will try to be the best woman I know I can be with you. So what I'm trying to say is…I love you too."

Brian gave me another passionate kiss and then flipped me ever so gently, positioning my buttocks upward. He removed my underwear with his teeth, just the way I like it. He then slid inside of me gently and slowly made love to me. The feeling of that moment was so romantic, I never wanted it to end.

Brian whispered in my ear which turned me on even more. "Baby, I love you. Promise me you'll never leave me."

I moaned with pleasure for he just felt so good inside of me. "I'll never leave you, baby. I promise. Me and you, always and f..f..f..forever," I said as I climaxed.

* * * *

When Brian tested the three magic words on Rita, he was afraid. Afraid that he would scare her away or that she would think that it would mean marriage as a next step. He wanted neither. But when she responded with an "I love you too," he was very pleased. She didn't get scared or consider it a future proposal. Now that he finally got those three words out of the way, he knew he would be stable for a while longer. He knew that she had been awaiting those words from him and knew his time was running out. He meant every word though; he really did love Rita and everything that came with the package, like the fact that he now had a roof over his head, food in his mouth, clothes on his back, jewelry on his hands and neck and a brand new Cadillac, thanks to his new woman. And now he was going to Disneyland, a place he'd been dying to visit every since he was five years old, her treat.

Nothing turned him on more than a woman who gave in to his every need. After seeing her poetry club, he knew she could easily afford to take care of him. The club was decorated with some of the most expensive furniture, lighting and flooring that Brian had ever seen.

While making love to Rita, Brian thought of how easy it was to get her to do whatever he asked of her, so long as he kept the charm rolling. He prayed his secrets wouldn't be revealed. Brian stared at Rita while he rocked her world. In his opinion, she wasn't as pretty as Leona, but she was beautiful. He remembered Rita mentioning a few months before that she wanted children and that almost scared him away. He made sure she took her birth control pills everyday. She had no idea that he knew where her stash was hidden and every day around 10:00 a.m., Brian checked to see if that day's pill had been popped. He couldn't reveal to Rita that he already had two children who lived in Texas. The order of protection from their mother was what prevented him from seeing them. There was no way he was going to bring another child in this world. Life sucked. And the only way he was going to have another child was when he fell in love. Yes, he loved Rita, but no, he was not *"in love"* with her. And, after his breakup with Leona, he vowed never to fall in love again.

* * * *

Chapter 8

Tonight was Soul Expression's annual black tie poetry slam. Brian and I walked into the jam-packed club arm in arm. As usual, all eyes were on us. I was looking very sexy that evening - dressed in a Ralph Lauren strapless grown contemplated with a pair of Jimmy Choo shoes, diamond choker and drop earrings, and my baby, Brian, was sporting a four-button Armani tuxedo with a satin notch lapel, a gift from me which was well worth it. We looked like we were dressed for the Emmy's.

"Brian, baby, why don't you have a seat at our table. I have to go to the office and make sure everything is in place for the big show."

Brian kissed me on my forehead. "Go ahead, baby. I'll be over there missing you every minute you're gone."

"You are too sweet. By the way, you're looking really handsome in that suit." And I meant every word of that statement.

Brian blushed. "Thanks for the suit, baby. I don't know what I would do without you. But your turn is next. When I get on my feet, I'm going to spoil you rotten."

"I just want my man to be happy," I sang as I walked towards my office." I couldn't wait for my turn to be spoiled. After all, that is what I'm accustomed to. I've always dated men who spoiled me with expensive gifts, not the other way around. "My baby will get on his feet soon," I thought to myself. "Hopefully, very soon."

* * * *

Brian walked towards his and Rita's table. They always sat at the head table by the stage. He was really starting to get into this poetry stuff, especially the black power pieces, and was looking forward to the show. At first, he thought that he would never get into poetry; that was why he hesitated to come to the club in the beginning of their courtship, but now, he was hooked and couldn't wait for the show to start.

While waiting, Brian's eyes roamed the club. There were many beautiful women in the club and a few of them noticed him also. He usually never paid the women at the club any special attention, but one woman in particular caught his eye. He had never seen her before. She was definitely not a regular at the club. She was beautiful - sort of favored Robin Givens only of a lighter complexion with twice the meat on her bones, just the way he liked his women. He noticed that she was sitting with a woman who could have passed for a twin sister, only the other woman seemed much older. He had to meet her. He remembered that Rita informed her bartender that all of his drinks were on the house. Brian walked over to the bar and ordered two dirty martinis. Since the waitresses were Rita's employees, he couldn't have them deliver the drinks to the ladies for fear that they would snitch, so he delivered the drinks himself. "Two dirty martini's for the beautiful ladies," he said as he placed the drinks in front of Sophie and Paulette.

"Sorry, sir, but we didn't order anything," Paulette said.

"They are on the house," Brian said as he locked eyes with Sophie.

"Are you the owner?" Sophie asked.

"No...well...I'm sort of dating the owner," Brian said. He saw the disappointed look in Sophie's eyes after he admitted to dating Rita. He had to come up with something fast before she lost her interest in him.

"You look like the kind of woman who appreciates art. Can I please leave you my number? I need an honest opinion on a piece I'm working on."

"So, you're an artist?" Paulette interrupted.

"Well, yes and no. You see, I'm new to the world of art so I'm just getting started. I only have a few paintings so far."

Brian's attention went back to Sophie. "May I just tell you that you are the most beautiful woman I've ever seen?"

Sophie blushed. "Why, thank you," she said. She knew she'd turn a few heads. The long-sleeved black criss-cross bodice gown by Michael Kors and "dominatrix" Manolo Blahnik heels made her look fabulous. She wanted to return the compliment of him being damn fine, but didn't want to say too much in front of her mother.

"My name is Brian. And yours?"

"Sophie, and this is my mother, Paulette Scott."

"Pleasure meeting the both of you."

Paulette turned her nose up at Brian. There was something about him that bugged her. Not only was he flirting shamelessly with her daughter, but his date was somewhere in the room not knowing what he was up to. But she hadn't seen Sophie smile in that way since meeting Ahmad so she excused herself to go to the ladies room to powder her nose. If a little flirting is what it took to put a smile on her baby's face, then so be it. She just prayed that her daughter wouldn't fall for him. She could spot a gigolo a mile away.

"Have a seat, Brian," Sophie gestured.

"Well, I can't sit long. I don't want to upset my date." Brian sat in the seat with his back towards Rita's office.

Sophie felt a tingly sensation when Brian stared at her. Not even Ahmad could make her feel this way. "So, this date of yours, where is she?"

"She's in the office setting things up for the evening."

"So, before she steals you away from me, are you going to give me that number or what? I would love to check out your artwork," Sophie said flirtatiously. She purposely tipped her purse onto the floor to bend over and give Brian a sneak peak of her cleavage. She hadn't felt this sexy in a while and something about him made her feel like a wild woman.

Brian noticed the cleavage alright. He also noticed the expensive dress, shoes and jewelry. And, to his satisfaction, there was no jewelry on her ring finger. "Before I give you that number, may I ask if you have a man?"

"I'm recently divorced and no, I'm not seeing anyone, not at the moment anyway."

Brian smiled as he stood from the table. "Well, if you ever want to see my artwork or just want to talk, give me a call." He handed Sophie one of his business cards which only displayed his name and cellular phone number.

Paulette returned to the table. Brian saw the unfavorable look she gave him. "Nice to meet you, Ms. Scott."

"Uh huh. I guess it's about time you got back to your date."

"Yes, mam." He winked at Sophie and walked back to his table.

Sophie gawked at her mother. "Mother, why were you so rude to him? He was just trying to be nice."

Paulette knew how weak her daughter was when it came to men. "Honey, I don't know about that one. If he can disrespect his date like he just did, what makes you think he won't eventually do that to you? You have to notice the little things like that when seeking love."

"I'm not trying to marry him mother? It was just harmless flirting, that's all."

"Uh huh, sure, harmless flirting. You're lucky his date didn't come out and harm you," she said with a chuckle in her voice. "Now, let's not argue and enjoy the rest of the evening."

Sophie and Paulette lifted their martini glasses to toast Sophie's escape from home. As she sipped her cocktail, her eyes roamed over to Brian's table. She noticed that he was staring at her, probably the whole time. She smiled, put her thumb and pinky finger up to her ear and mouthed the words "*I'll call you.*"

* * * *

Chapter 9

I watched the whole encounter – from the time Brian walked away from our table to him handing some sort of business card to that hoochie mama. The jealousy and rage I felt within myself overpowered the love I felt for him. When Brian returned to our table, I composed myself and went over to join him. For the first time, I could not look straight into my man's eyes.

"Hey! I missed you!" Brian said as he stood to embrace me.

Seated only a few feet away, I'd seen how that woman purposely waited for my man to look in her direction to demonstrate how to suck every ounce of juice from the olive of her martini. The older woman was doing her thing on the dance floor with a gentleman half her age. I also noticed the quick smile Brian gave her before he turned his attention back to me.

I hunched over so that the anger displayed on my face would not be seen by the crowd. "You missed me huh! So, you missed me so much that you gave your telephone number to another woman?" I wanted to yell at him, but instead I chose a high-pitch whisper. There was no way I was going to embarrass myself in my own establishment.

Brian cringed. *"Damn, how in the hell did she see me?"* He rarely got caught doing things like this and when he did, he wanted to slap himself. "Baby, come on now. That was my...um...an old high school friend of mine."

"A high school friend? You could do better than that, Brian!"

"Baby, why would I lie to you? You want to go over there and ask her?"

"Well, if she's an old high school friend, then why couldn't you just say, *"Hi. Nice to see you."* Why did you give her your number? Why do you want her to call you?"

Brian, seeing that his lie was working, continued on. "Baby, she has a friend who owns a construction company and I gave her my card to pass on to him. I thought it would be good to talk to him to see how I can get things started for myself."

I stared at Brian for at least ten seconds trying to determine if what he says is the truth. I wanted to trust him, but his lies in the beginning of our relationship made it hard for me, especially with his not working and driving that horrific car. But after looking deeply into his eyes, I decided to let it go; besides, I couldn't help that I had the best-looking man in the whole club. No wonder that woman couldn't keep her eyes off my man. He looked like a million bucks tonight in his tux. "Okay, okay, I'm tripping. I'm sorry for not believing you. I guess I got a little jealous. You know I want you all to myself."

"A little jealous? Girl, you were ready to take off your nails and shoes and beat her down!"

I shoved him playfully. "Shut up. It's just that I love you and I want us to grow together. You're good for me. I just wished that your luck will get better in making some money for yourself. Tell you what, how about after the show, you and I discuss you working for me as one of my managers here."

"I'm sorry, Rita, but the last thing I want to do is work for my woman. I really want to open my own construction company, and all I need is fifty thousand to start it off. I'm going to get my proposal together and see if there is one bank out there who will give a little something something to a brother."

"Fifty Thousand? Wow. Well, if you can't get that loan, then let me know. I may be able to help you out a little. But, Brian, if I do this for you, I am going to expect every last penny back within one year. I will be jeopardizing the club if I don't get it back."

"You will do that for me?"

"Maybe. Just see what the banks tell you first." I instantly regretted making that offer to him and truly don't know why I did. I had to have been whipped. I had yet again, put my foot in my mouth. I was pissed at myself, but that is just how I am. My middle name should have been "Salvation Army". I was really generous when it came to helping people out, but nothing as much as a $50,000 loan. Damn, I must really be in love.

My patrons were getting impatient. It was time to start the grand show. Brian was still in la la land from me offering him the loan. I interrupted his goofy smile. "The show is starting. I have to introduce the first poet." I walked on the stage and received a big round of applause. "Thank you. Thank you very much. First of all, I want to thank each and every last one of you for coming out for the Soul Expressions black tie poetry slam. Everyone looks like a million bucks!" Another round of applause. "Now, the time has arrived for our first poet to perform. Please show your love for......me!" The crowd loved when I surprised them with a special piece of my own. They applauded. Then, everything went silent which is one of the major rules at Soul Expressions. No talking during spoken word. "This poem is dedicated to a very special friend of mine. He knows who he is." I glanced at Brian and prepared to do my special piece, written exclusively for him, "Blind Date":

Butterflies in My Lower Abdomen
Picturing the perfect image of masculinity
Are you the love that I longed for? Prayed for?
Your physical identity I imagine is as your voice
Deep, seductive, sexy, inspiring...
Is your complexion as deep as your words?
Chocolate, caramel or french vanilla will do...
Are your teeth as white as your spirit?

Clean, saved, holy, renewed?
Are your lips as full as your heart?
Which is what got my attention from the start...
Your words to me shows me you know how to love
Your words - those beautiful words - caused my attraction
to you
I can think of
No one but you
Are you the soul mate I'm craving to find?
Did my God send you to me at a time
In my life
That I need to receive love? Give love?
The time is here after hearing only your voice
My choice is no matter what your physical appearance
reflects
I am going to love you!
Your words have captured me
But we'll put them to the test
To see if your attitude towards me is as beautiful as you
suggest
Through your words
You have been all that and more
And no matter what happens, I will always adore you
Peace

I received a standing ovation, including Brian, who clapped louder than anyone. I smiled as I was pleased that he enjoyed it. After the crowd settled down, I introduced the next poet and walked back to my table to sit with Brian.

* * * *

Sophie watched the infamous Rita as she recited her poem to Brian. *"That poem wasn't all that,"* she thought to herself. *"What is it that he sees in her? She's not as pretty as I am."* Although Brian was not her man, Sophie found herself getting a little jealous as she watched the affection between the two of them. She missed that feeling of belonging to someone, lovemaking...basically, the feeling of being complete and settled. Each time she saw Rita and Brian kiss, hold hands and Rita straightening Brian's tie, she pictured herself in Rita's shoes.

Maxximus, who was another one of Soul Expression's famous poets, was introduced as the next poet. His poems were of a romantic nature and the women always paid close attention whenever he recited. He performed his famous piece, *The Joshua Tree*:

> *Another place...*
> *Another time...*
> *Meet me at the Joshua Tree*
> *You tell your secrets...*
> *I'll tell you mine*
> *...and we'll settle down in the barren desert*
> *to listen to the music of Nature's call*
> *if Nature chooses to sing at all*
> *We'll make love amid the rock formations*
> *and dance upon the canyon floor...*
> *We'll build a campfire and gaze at the stars*
> *that beckon from the sky above*
> *and we'll forget that we have troubles*
> *waiting for us back there*
> *in that "other" world...*
> *Where sirens scream*
> *bill collectors call and chaos waits*

> *like a predator in the darkened*
> *corners*
> *of the room...*
> *Meet me at the Joshua Tree*
> *and if I don't make it...*
> *light a candle in my memory*
> *to honor the desert winds*
> *that brought us together beneath its*
> *azure skies*

Paulette interrupted her daughter's thoughts with her loud clapping. "Wow, that was beautiful! Did you like that piece?"

"Huh? Oh, sorry mother, I wasn't paying attention," said Sophie. She knew that the sexy poet spoke of something about meeting him at the Joshua Tree. She spent the rest of the evening thinking of her and Brian, only she had to remember that Brian was not her man – not yet. *Yeah, Brian, meet me at the Joshua Tree so I can show you what I got.*

* * * *

Three hours later, the show had finally ended. Brian was relieved. He couldn't wait for the next day to call Sophie and see what she was all about. He hardly paid any attention to any of the other poets because he thought of Sophie for the rest of the evening and how he could work his magic on her all night. Though he was satisfied with just being with Rita, there was something special about Sophie that made him crave her -- maybe it was because Sophie's physique reminded him so much of Leona.

Sophie and her mother gathered their coats and proceeded to the door. Sophie spotted Rita and Brian standing by the front entrance. She straightened her posture and walked her sexiest walk, hoping Brian would notice. She purposely bumped into Brian on her way out the door. "Oh, excuse me, Brian."

"That's quite alright. It was a pleasure meeting you and I'll give you a call about that business proposal," he said as he gave Sophie a look that let her know that he wanted her.

* * * *

I didn't miss a beat. Every second of that encounter pissed me off. I gave Sophie my best phony smile. "Hope you enjoyed your evening," I interrupted.

"Oh, I did…very much," Sophie said to me while smiling at Brian.

I wanted to slap the shit out of Sophie, but I contained my emotions due to other customers still hanging around.

Paulette interrupted. "Well, we had a wonderful evening. I look forward to hearing the beautiful poetry again next week. Sophie, are you ready to go now?"

"Yes, mother. We can go now. Bye Brian," she sang.

Brian held the door open for Sophie and he gave her a friendly smile as she walked out of the club.

*　*　*　*

Paulette grabbed Sophie's arm as soon as they reached the parking lot. "What did you think you were doing in there, Sophie? I've never been so embarrassed in my life!"

Sophie knew that her mother wouldn't let her get away with her rude behavior. "What are you talking about, mother?" she asked innocently.

Paulette's face was red with anger. "Sophie, let me tell you something right now. That was totally disrespectful of one sister to another. Why did you have to flirt with that man right in front of his girlfriend? That is not like you, Sophie. What is really going on?"

"Mom, oh, come on, please, give me a break. Look at what happened to me and Ahmad. Look at how these women stole my man. Why can't I be the woman who takes another woman's man? It always happens to me. I've been nice my whole life and never ever disrespected anyone. It's women like Rita and all of these other hoochies out here who think they can just come into my life, take my man and ruin me. This time it's my turn."

"Oh, Sophie, Sophie, Sophie. That woman in there didn't take Ahmad from you. You can't just do that to people. Believe me, Ahmad will reap what he sows." She hugged her daughter. Look, baby, I see you're still hurting over him, but you need to get over it, get back into the church and start a whole new life without him. There are plenty of available men out here and you don't have to go after anyone. In due time, the Lord will send you that special someone."

"But mom…"

"But mom, nothing. Look, baby, the way Brian was flirting with you in front of her, what makes you think he won't disrespect you like that with another woman in the future if you ever did quote, unquote, "win" him?"

"Mother, I'm attracted to Brian. I know I just met him, but it's been five months since I've been with anyone! Five months! And it's hard for me to just go out and meet a man like him. It's like love at first sight or something and I haven't felt this way in a long time about anyone. Besides, I don't have time to wait for the love of my life, I want to get what I want and get it now. I know I was wrong tonight, but the way Ahmad played me, I feel like a totally different woman now. I want a challenge! It's time for revenge!"

"Oh, baby," Paulette sighed. "It's your life. You're an adult and I can't tell you how to live it. But just be careful and whatever you do, get back into the church and maybe your mind will change with God."

They got into the car. Sophie decided not to spark up the conversation again and turned up the car radio. Paulette, also not wanting to continue the conversation, was saying a long, silent prayer for her daughter throughout the whole drive.

* * * *

After Sophie and her mother left the club, Brian saw that I was upset. He knew he went too far with the flirting this time.

"Baby. It's not what you think."

I walked away because I refused to argue with my man in the presence of others, but I couldn't wait to get to the car to give him a piece of my mind. I advised my manager to make sure the club was spotless for tomorrow night's show and to lock up once everything was cleaned up. "Brian, are you ready?" I asked nonchalantly. I tried to remain calm.

"Yeah, sweetie. Go ahead to the car. I have to go to the men's room first." Brian headed towards the restroom to hide the telephone number that Sophie slipped in his pant pocket on her way out.

I got into the car and was trying my best to calm down. *Please don't tell me I've wound up with another dog. I thought he was different! I bought that dog a car! How could he do this to me!*

A few minutes later, Brian interrupted my thoughts as he got in the car and gave me a kiss. "I love you and only you. Don't be like that," he said.

"Brian, please! You were flirting with her just as much as she was flirting with you! How dare you do that to me after all I've done for you!"

"Look, baby. Women flirt. I can't help it that they flirt with me! I don't want to be with anybody else but you! Don't you see that!"

"Whatever, Brian! I am not the one to play with! If you are going to be with me, then don't...."

Brian grabbed me by the throat.

"Look! I am a grown ass man and don't appreciate being talked to like that!" he screamed.

"Let me go, Brian!" I was in total shock by his abusive behavior and I didn't know what to do. His hands stayed put on my throat for a few seconds longer before he released it. It took me a few seconds to regain my breathing. *Breathe in... breathe out... Breathe in... breathe out. Now get the fuck away from this crazy deranged psycho!*

Before I could reach for the door handle, Brian started in with his apologies.

"I'm sorry, baby. I didn't mean..."

I had to snap. I couldn't just let it go. "You didn't mean to what? To choke me? What the fuck was that all about? What in the hell did you think you were doing? Are you some kind of sick monster or something? Do you realize that you could have killed me?"

Brian's tone matched mine. "Look, damn it! What do you want from me? I'm doing the best I can here! Can't you see that I love you? Can't we just go home and forget about this?"

"Brian, if you loved me, then why did you put your hands on me? Do you have a history with abusing women or something?" I was still lacking airwaves. My neck felt like a pound of concrete fell onto it. The pain only made me angrier. "And, no, we cannot just go home! What is going on? First you flirt with another woman in my face and now this...this...choking thing?"

"Rita! Look, I'm sorry. I'm just really frustrated right now!"

"Frustrated about what, Brian! Frustrated about lying to me? Frustrated about living in *My* house, eating *My* food, spending *My* money...living a life of luxury and not having to lift a finger?"

Brian was angry. He knew he was somewhat of a gigolo, but he didn't want it thrown in his face, and Rita made sure to throw it in his face every chance she got. Back in the day, he used to think that it made him less of a man, but nowadays, he considered it being a player. And if she knew what he was doing to her, then why did she continue to see him? Everything about that moment reminded him of Leona and how she too would say things like that to him. "Rita, if you don't put this car in drive and get me home now, you are going to regret it!"

"Regret it! What is that suppose to mean, Brian?"

"Drive! Now!"

His tone was evil and I didn't want to get him any angrier. My past lover had the same evilness about him. I put the car in drive and headed home. There were no words spoken between us for the entire ride. I was afraid and now I had a serious headache and a serious case of jitters. Because of my last relationship, I knew what would come next if I said another word to him. After a long silent ride, I pulled up into my driveway, got out of the car, slowly walked up to the door and unlocked it. Once in the house, I panicked and ran upstairs to my bedroom and locked the door behind me.

Brian chased me, but failed to catch up. My being on the track team in high school really paid off.

"Rita, open the door!"

"No!"

Brian experienced de'ja' vu. This moment reminded Brian of Leona and how she too would lock herself in her bedroom. Rita's stubbornness was wearing his patience. "Open the damn door!"

"You have to calm down first, Brian! You are scaring me!"

"Oh, I'm scaring you! You're scaring me! You're not calling the police are you?"

"Police? No, I didn't call the police!" *Why on earth is he asking that?* "I am going to open this door and when I do, you'd better not try anything!"

"Come on, open the door!" Every second of this drama was heightening his anger.

I finally opened the door and as soon as I poked my head out, Brian slapped me across my right eye. "Ouch! Brian, no!" I felt like I was playing the lead role in a Lifetime movie.

Brian froze. He didn't mean to do that, but his anger took over. "Damn, baby, I am so sorry. I don't know what's happening to me. Are you okay?"

I curled on my bed and cried. "Leave me alone! Why are you doing this to me?" I cried. I never understood what men got out of hurting women and I never wanted to understand.

"Oh, baby. I'm sorry. It won't happen again, ever. I'm sorry." Brian curled behind me and held me tightly. He kissed me softly on my right cheek and apologized over and over again. My eye was starting to pound. I was afraid of what it may look like in the morning. I turned to face Brian and the look on his face confirmed that my eye wasn't a pretty site.

Brian kissed my eye. "Does that make it feel better."

"I'm okay, Brian," I said as the tears ran down my face. He seemed so sincere when he kissed my eye. Made me feel like a baby who had a little boo boo that could be fixed with just a peck. "Why did you hit me? What have I done?"

"Nothing. You did absolutely nothing," said Brian. "I just get angry sometimes and my temper sometimes gets out of control. That's not how I am though; I don't hit women. I don't know what's gotten into me this evening. I'm sorry again and again and again, okay?"

I again heard the sincerity in his voice. Not even my ex showed that much compassion when apologizing. I wanted to believe him. I stared at

Brian which instantly brought a smile to my wet face. "Okay."

Brian lowered his voice into a sexy and seductive tone. "Do you still love me?"

"Yes I do…. just promise me that you won't hurt me again."

Brian smiled. "I promise, baby. I promise."

* * *

Chapter 10

The next day, Brian and I held hands through Magic Kingdom. The trip to Florida was getting a bit expensive. Brian wanted to go to almost every park Florida had to offer and the admission fees were very costly. He acted as if I had money coming out of my ears or something, but it was my fault - I spoiled him. I really wanted to go home. I had been to Disneyland 50,000 times already and it just wasn't fun anymore for me. Brian, on the other hand, acted as if he were a 7-year old kid who had never stepped foot out of the house.

There was one particular moment when I thought that he was going to bankrupt me. We were just getting off the Pirates of the Caribbean, which is one of Disney's most popular rides, when Brian spotted an advertisement for the Granada Gallery. I didn't know what had gotten into him, but he pretty much demanded that we tour the gallery. I told him that I wasn't into all of that art stuff and it surprised me that he had such a hard on for it. He acted as if his life depended on visiting this place so I gave in and agreed to go. When we finally arrived at the art gallery, which took us more than an hour by taxi, Brian rushed in ahead of me. "Um, hello!" I said. "Remember me?" I felt like an abandoned child.

Brian caught himself and gave me a look of embarrassment. "Oh, I'm sorry, baby. I didn't mean to leave you like that." He walked back to me and took me by the hand.

A couple who were holding hands walked by us with smirks on their faces. I wanted to stick my tongue out at them, but that would have shown my immature side. "What's up with all the rushing? Are you that excited about art?"

"Well, yeah!" he said.

"Since when were you so interested in art? You never mentioned it to me."

"Let's just go inside and see what they have, alright? Don't start!"

He shut me up quick. The look he gave me was similar to the evil look he had last night in the car. I grabbed his hand to calm him down. We walked hand in hand throughout the gallery. In my opinion, most of the art was horrendous, but Brian took his time looking around as if every piece was a masterpiece. One painting in particular, caught his eye.

"This is it! Buy this one for me!" he said out of nowhere.

"Excuse me?"

"I want this one!"

"Brian, do I look like your mother? I am not paying $4,000 for a painting!"

"Come on Rita! I'll pay you back, I promise."

And that's when I lost it. "Brian, when you get a job, then you can pay for the damn thing yourself! How could you ask me to purchase something like that for that kind of money?"

"Rita, if you're not going to buy it, then just say no. There is no need to get an attitude about it!"

"I am not buying that painting, Brian!"

"Fine!"

Brian walked out of the gallery and left me standing there with my mouth hung open. I yelled after him. "Brian!"

He turned around and gave me a look of disappointment. "What!"

"What is wrong with you?"

"Nothing!"

"Don't tell me nothing, Brian! I paid for this trip, the clothes you're wearing on this trip, the shoes you're walking around in on this trip and not to mention, the car you drove us to the airport in. And all you got to say is nothing?"

"So, you're just going to throw that in my face? Do you want me to give it all back, Rita? You act like all I care about is your money. I love you, baby. You! I don't give a damn about your money!"

I felt bad. Brian was so pissed off at me. "I'm sorry, baby. I didn't mean to rub it in. Look, if you want the painting, then…"

Brian cut me off. "No….never mind," he said. "You're right. It is a bit expensive. But thanks anyway. Come on, let's just go to Animal Kingdom and have some more fun."

"Brian, I thought we were only going to spend a day here. It's already 4:00 and I booked our flight for 8:00 tonight. I don't think we have time for Animal Kingdom. I really have to get back to the club."

"You're not enjoying yourself?" asked Brian. I'm having a ball. I've always wanted to come out here."

"I am having fun, but…" I decided not to start another argument with Brian. It would definitely set him off this time because I haven't been very agreeable with him all day. It wasn't as if I needed another black eye or bruised neck. I had to wear sunglasses the whole trip to cover the lump under my eye. I believed Brian when he apologized for last night, but I didn't know if I trusted his promise of not hitting me again. I've heard that sad song before; the difference between Brian and my ex, Keith, was that Brian was a site for sore eyes while Keith caused sore eyes if you sighted him, cause Keith was sho nuff an ugly brother. And the other difference was that Keith would have paid for this damn boring trip.

I didn't know how I was going to hide these bruises when I got back to work; I would probably have to pile on the makeup which would surprise everyone since I hardly wore more than eyeliner and lipstick.

After our fight last night, Brian reminded me that I was taking him to Disneyland in the morning. I was kind of blown away by his persistence, but a promise was a promise and I'd promised him that we would go.

"But what!" he said, scaring my thoughts away.

Brian seemed as if he wanted to start an argument with me. He started to remind me of Lawrence Fishburne when he played Ike in *"What's Love Got to Do With It"*. "Nothing," I said. I gave him my best smile to let him know that everything was fine. "Let's just try and enjoy the rest of the trip, okay? We could leave tomorrow morning."

"That's what I'm talking about, baby. You need this get-a-way. And again, about last night…I'm sorry…"

"Brian, please. Let's just forget about it."

"Let me finish," Brian said. "Rita, I can't live without you. I'm sorry for the way things went down. I want you to forgive me so we could move on. So, do you forgive me? I mean, really forgive me?"

I wanted to forgive him, but my mind kept telling me not to. My body, on the other hand, didn't want to let go. He was the greatest lover I ever had. I figured since I had already invested five months of my life into this relationship, then I might as well keep it going. Although I'd gotten accustomed to being alone, something about having someone to come home to made me feel needed, wanted and loved. I missed my mother. She died alone though. Although I was there by her bedside, she was still lonely. My mother's whole life story could be summed up in one sentence: "She lived to get married, but failed". The topic of most of her conversations were about finding a husband for herself. Didn't matter that she had me; she wanted a man in her life. I didn't want to leave this world feeling like she had.

My eyes filled with tears. "Baby, we'll get through this. There's no one in the world I'd rather spend my time with."

"I feel the same way," he said.

I grabbed Brian's hand and we headed out to the streets to flag down a cab. "I'm getting really tired. Is it okay if we head back to the room now?"

Brian looked down at his watch. They had been walking and getting on rides for more than five hours now and the cab ride to the gallery did make him a little sleepy. "Yeah, sure," he said.

Once we were in our hotel suite, I started to remove my clothing. I was feeling really funky from all of that walking. It had to be 100 degrees outside. "I want to take a bubble bath, do you want to join me?"

"Yeah, but you go ahead and I'll be in there in a second."

Brian waited until I rested in the bathtub, then walked back towards the bed, looking a little suspicious.

"I have to make a telephone call," he said. "Be in there in a sec!"

The water was a little too hot, so I got up and cracked the door, leaving it open just enough to catch a cold breeze while I soaked.

* * * *

Chapter 11

Sophie's heart skipped a beat at the sound of the ringing telephone. She had been expecting Brian's call all day and crossed her fingers, hoping it was him. "Hello," she said in her sexiest voice.

"Hi. May I please speak with Sophie?"

"This is she." She recognized that voice anywhere. It was Brian. "Hello, Brian."

"How are you, Sophie? I was wondering if you're still interested in checking out my artwork?"

"Actually, I'm interested in checking out more than your artwork," Sophie teased.

"Is that right?"

"Yes, that's right." Sophie lied down on her satin sheets. His voice could charm the panties off of her. "It shows on my caller id that you are calling from an out of area location. Are you out of town?"

"Yes, well, I'm stuck in Florida, but I should be returning home by tomorrow evening."

"Are you out there on business or pleasure?"

"Business. I'm actually meeting with a few art dealers who may, in the future, host an art show for me."

"Sounds like a man who knows what he wants and how to get it," she teased.

"Well, that would be me. So, is it okay if I stopped by tomorrow night at 8:00?"

"Make it 7:00. I can't wait to see you...I mean, your artwork."

* * * *

I, while soaking in my bubble bath, could not believe my ears. *Did he say artwork? Out here on business?* I can't believe him! I recognized Sophie's name from the club and that pissed me off even more. "Brian!" I yelled. I wanted to make sure that Sophie heard my voice on the other end. "Are you going to join me in this hot bubble bath or what!" There! That would show her what type of business he was on.

Sophie heard the voice in the background. "Brian, who was that?"

"I gotta go, Sophie. I'll see you tomorrow. Bye now."

Brian hung up the telephone and walked into the bathroom. "Just let me get out of these clothes and I'll be right in, baby."

"Don't bother!" I said as I stepped out of the tub and charged past him.

"Well, I guess I'll have to soak by myself," he said as he undressed and closed the door. "I don't know what's gotten into you, but I hope you're not mad again!" he yelled through the door.

"Why wouldn't I be mad?" I thought. Enough was enough. I was going to stop this woman right now. I walked straight to the telephone and dialed the operator. "Yes, operator, can you please redial the last number called from this room?"

I dug my nails into the wooden dresser next to the bed. This bitch had to go and I couldn't wait to give her a piece of my mind.

* * * *

Sophie, seeing the out of area call on her caller id, ran to the phone. "Out of area again. That's got to be Brian." She picked up the telephone smiling the biggest smile ever. "Hello again, Brian."

"This is not Brian! This is Brian's girlfriend! Stay the hell away from my man!" I wanted to say more, but the last time I had to confront another woman was back in high school. My mind went blank.

Sophie was also shocked. She had never received a telephone call like this one, but remembered saying the same thing to Ahmad's mistresses. "Is this Rita?"

"How did you know my name?"

Sophie would repeat the same thing Ahmad's other women would say to her. "If he were your man, then he wouldn't be coming after me!"

I was appalled! How dare this woman admit to wanting my man! What has this world come to? "Look, I'm going to tell you one more time, stay away from Brian!"

Sophie found this situation very humorous. "No, bitch! You stay away from *my* man!" And with that, Sophie hung up.

What the hell? I was confused, yet pissed. "Are the women that desperate nowadays?" I said to no one in particular.

"Rita! Who are you talking to!" Brian yelled from the bathroom.

"No one!" I was still confused, but it only took a second to come to a resolution. I had to be crazy to think that I would fight over a man who couldn't even buy me a tube of socks. And arguing with another woman for any man was a no no in my book. I made a decision right then and there that I would let Brian go. Give him the peace sign and continue on with my life - something I should have done the moment he put his hands on me. Hell, if I have to be lonely, then so be it. And as soon as I get back to sweet home Chicago, I am definitely removing my profile from singleblackworld.com. There was no way I was ever going to try internet dating again. Not if it came with all of this drama.

Brian walked out of the bathroom. "What was that all about? Why didn't you stay in the tub with me?"

"Brian, we need to talk," I said.

"Here we go again! How many times I gotta tell you that I was sorry for…"

"Brian, no, it's not just about that!"

"Then, what is it?"

"Everything! I can't do this anymore!"

"You can't do what anymore!"

"I can't be with you!"

Brian let out a hearty laugh. "Girl, you must be crazy. I'm not going anywhere!"

"What do you mean, you're not going anywhere! I want out of this! I don't want to be with you! Oh, and I heard you on the telephone! I even called her. Apparently after only five months, you decide that you want to cheat on me!"

"You called who?" Brian asked.

"I called Sophie."

"Why in the world did you do that?"

"Because I needed to know if you were really the liar I thought you were!"

Brian's mind went wild. *I hope she didn't mess up my chances with Sophie.* "What did you say to her?" he asked.

"I told her to stay away from you, but I guess she made up her mind that you're worth fighting for and, baby, I refuse to fight over you!" Truth be told, I really didn't want to let him go, but there was no way I was going to fight for him. The dick wasn't that good. Okay, yes it was, but still, I wasn't going to share it.

"You won't fight for me? A lot of women would fight to keep me!"

"Yes, I can see that. But you got the wrong one this time. Ms. Sophie can have your sorry ass."

Why in the hell did I say that? What happened next left me in a total state of confusion. Brian charged at me as if he were tackling a football player and ran me into the wall. He then picked me up by my collar and threw me over the bed. My head hit the edge of the drawer, causing blood to race past my eye and onto the white towel wrapped around me. "Brian, no!" I screamed. And if that wasn't enough, he stood over me and kicked me in my stomach. I cringed with pain.

"Like, I said, I'm not going anywhere. And, if you think you're going to get rid of me, then think again, bitch!" Brian stormed out of the hotel room.

I curled on the carpeting and cried like my life was over. *Why me? How did I get myself into this again?* I hated myself for being so stupid. Even after all of this, I stilled loved him. I went to the bathroom to clean myself up. Now, not only did I have a lump under my eye, but now another one forming on my forehead, not to mention that my neck was still sore from last night's episode. I wanted to run away from everything. No matter what my heart tells me and no matter what he says, I was not going to allow him to ruin my life. I walked back into the bedroom with an ice pack in hand and placed it on my forehead. What I should have done was packed my shit and got the hell out of Florida at that moment, but I didn't want to leave him stranded. My heart has always been that way. I was a caring person – no matter what.

I was surprised by Brian's actions and never expected for him to threaten me when I wanted to end the relationship. No matter how many times he apologized, I had to convince myself not to forgive him this time. I was smart enough to get out of my relationship with Keith and, no matter what, I can get myself out of this one with Brian.

An hour passed before Brian walked back into the hotel suite with a bouquet of roses in hand. I could not believe that he had the audacity to buy me roses, especially with my own money. Brian didn't have a dime to contribute to this trip so he had to have purchased those roses with the credit card I gave him yesterday. That only made me angrier. It was then that I realized that I was just a little too damn generous with him.

I didn't look at him when he walked towards me. I was truly disgusted. Did he actually think that a bunch of funky ass roses would heal this situation? Who does he think he is? *There was no way I would forgive him. There was no damn way I would forgive him. There was absolutely no fucking way I was going to forgive his ass* -that's what I had to keep telling myself. Hell, we hadn't even been together that long. I had no ties to this man; no papers keeping him with me, except for the car which had both of our signatures on it. How could I have been so stupid?

Brian sat on the bed next to me. He choked up a few tears before speaking. "Baby, please don't let me go. I didn't mean to do this again. I love you and the thought of us not being together will kill me."

I didn't say one word. Nothing he could say would change anything. And at that moment, I wished someone would kill his ass. The tears did soften me up a little, but I had to be strong. *Do not forgive him. Do not forgive him damn it! Do not fucking forgive his ass* – remember, I curse a lot when I'm nervous! And Brian was making me nervous being all in my face -- smelling good, looking good, touching my hair.........*do not fucking forgive his ass!*

"Did you hear me baby?" Brian asked.

Yes, I heard him, but I stayed strong. I never responded.

* * * *

Brian was starting to doubt himself. He had already lost Leona and now it seemed as if he were about to lose Rita as well.

He didn't enjoy hitting on women, but he couldn't help it. While growing up, Brian saw a few fights between his mom and dad, only they didn't know he'd witnessed them. He had a secret hiding place whenever they fought and would peek out of the closet's keyhole only to see his father beat on his mother. Although he didn't agree with what his father did to his mother, Brian figured that it was the way marriage was suppose to be because his mother never gave a hint of wanting to leave his dad. But now that he was all grown up, he knew that he had a problem.

Brian walked out of the hotel suite to think things over. He was so angry with himself. Rita was a good woman, and not to mention, the only woman who ever wanted to help him with his dream of becoming an entrepreneur. There was not one woman in his life who went as far as even throwing him a penny when it came to his dreams, but never hesitated to buy him clothing and things just to show him off. He had to think of a way to keep her because she would be the key to his success - his last hope. He didn't want to wind up back in his mother's house, disappointing her yet once again. He dug deep into his pockets and retrieved Rita's credit card and headed towards Frederick's of Hollywood to find the perfect lingerie for her. All women loved lingerie, didn't they? That would probably cheer her up.

He also decided to find a store to find a painting to show Sophie when he met with her, something a lot cheaper than $4,000, and something that wouldn't make Rita's eyes buck out when she received her monthly statement. He still had to have something to show Sophie when he showed up at her place. He had no clue as to why he told Sophie he was an artist - that lie was going to be hard to play out. Sophie seemed like the type of woman who would believe his every word anyway, by the way she practically threw herself at him. He wasn't trying to risk his relationship with Rita, but he needed a backup – just in case things didn't turn out the way he planned. And if things did turn out good with Rita, then the both of them sharing him would be no problem. He felt like a kid again.

* * * *

Chapter 12

I packed the last of my things before Brian and I headed to the airport. Even after Brian presented me with a gift from a lingerie store purchased with my credit card, I still refused to say another word to him, although he looked kind of cute when he presented me with the beautifully wrapped box. I snatched it out of his hands and threw it over the bed though, just to show him that I was still upset.

Just so I can set the record straight, I wasn't trying to buy Brian, I just wanted to show him that money didn't mean much to me and that I didn't mind sharing it with the person I loved. I remembered when I was stone broke back in the day. I remembered thinking that when I open my poetry club, I'll have all the money in the world and then I'll be happy. And when I did open my poetry club, I had money pouring in from every which way, but still, I wasn't happy. So since then, I realized what was truly important to me – love with a capital "L".

I wanted to reach out to him and ask him over and over again why he couldn't control his temper, but that would be a waste of time. For some reason, even after his whooping my ass, there was still a lot of love in my heart for him.

Do not forgive his ass!

I was starting to think of my old, lonely, boring and single life.

Do not forgive his ass!

Okay, I'm fine now. I don't know what's happening with me. I am probably the most whipped female in the whole world. But I'll get over it. Sophie could have his ass. It would serve her right to try and steal somebody's man without knowing what life was like behind closed doors.

Brian couldn't take the fact that I was giving him the silent treatment.

"Baby, please, talk to me," he pleaded. "Please, say something! Anything!"

I could no longer hold in my silence. "What is it that you want from me, Brian? How can I ever face my staff and friends with these markings on my face?"

"I am going to seek counseling for this, Rita. I promise."

Brian broke down in real tears. Real tears! I couldn't help it, I broke down with him. My tears almost drowned me. "Why?" I cried.

"There are a lot of things that I need to explain to you… "Rita, I had an awful childhood and all I know is how my father treated my mother. But I can't do this anymore! I have to get help or I'll never forgive myself for doing this to you," he cried.

"It's not the first time, is it? Have you done this to anyone else in the past?"

Brian knew that his "dramatic" crying act would work like a charm. It always did – well, excluding the last incident with Leona. He continued on crying. "Rita, I've never really had a relationship. You are the first woman that I've ever fell in love with and the thought of you leaving me is the reason why I did what I did. I don't want to lose you."

My heart softened again, but still, I stayed strong. "Brian, how do you expect for me to want to be with you after what happened? I can't do this. No matter what happens, I can't be with you."

"Rita, please. One more chance. Just give me one more chance. Please!"

He sat down on the bed next to me, making sure to rub his skin against my skin which he knew turned me on all the way.

Do not fucking forgive his ass!

Then he grabbed my cheeks and forced me to look into his pretty eyes. He was so gorgeous.

Do not fucking forgive his ass!

Brian continued with his pleading. "Rita, I know you're tired of hearing me apologize." He took a deep breath. "I am going to get through this, baby. Can you please give me just one more itty bitty chance? Maybe help me find someone to talk to about this? Can we do this together, Rita?" Deep down inside, Brian was serious, but he knew damn well that he wasn't going to anyone's psychiatrist. He would work it out on his own.

Boy, he was really laying it on me. "Brian, it sounds like *you* need to talk to someone about that. I'm not the one who can't keep my hands to myself. It's not my problem, it's yours. We are not married, so why should I take time out of my schedule to accompany you to some psychiatrist?"

"Because, I love you and want to marry you," he said regretfully.

I froze. "What did you say?"

Brian swallowed his pride to repeat that awful statement. He knew he wasn't ready for another engagement, but if it would keep Rita around and her $50,000 offer, then he had to do what he had to do. He looked Rita straight into her eyes and swallowed his pride. "Rita, I want to marry you. I love you. When I get this company rolling, everything you've done for me will be given back to you and then some. I've never felt this way about anyone else and I want to show you how much I appreciate everything you do for me. And that means seeking help to control my temper. Whatever it takes!"

I had never received a marriage proposal before, but this is not how I planned it would happen. I wanted to be dressed in a satin gown, sitting in a meadow picnicking with my man when he pulls out this huge diamond and proposes to me, then laying me down on white sheets and us making love amidst tall dandelions. Okay, that was a little to fairytale-ish, but that is the kind of proposal I wanted. Though it felt good to hear the words, "marry me", there was still something that he didn't explain to me. "What about Sophie? What was that all about with you being out here on business and her telling me that you were her man?"

"I had to lie to her because I needed that hook up with the construction company owner. That woman is after me, but I don't pay her any attention. She'll never open my eyes like you do."

"And you being an artist?" I grilled.

"Er...um...well, I didn't want to tell her that I was unemployed. I'm kind of ashamed about that."

Brian had me on an emotional roller coaster. "Brian, I don't know. Maybe we can see what happens after your sessions are over with, but, I've been through this before and..."

Brian interrupted. "Can't you see I'm begging? I'm on my knees here begging you to give me one more chance and to be my wife. Please, don't mess up what we have. I need you!" Brian dropped to his knees and began to cry. "Rita...please...don't do this..."

What else could I do? I sensed true sincerity in his apology, but he had apologized before and now here I am looking like a feather weight getting knocked out by Mike Tyson. I didn't trust him; probably never would. He was so friggin' convincing at times. I didn't say a word – just stared at the top of his head in total confusion.

Brian looked up at me.

"So, baby, are you going to give me another shot? This is it for me. I can't stand seeing you hurt like this. Please?"

That was when my heart melted for him. I tried to keep my heart icy cold, but his tears always seemed to light a fire under it. I hoped I didn't regret saying what I was going to say next. "Okay, Brian, one more chance. Just one more."

My mother probably rolled over in her grave 50 times for my actions, and at this moment, I wished she were here to guide me and slap some sense into my head.

Brian's face lit up. What was it with a crying man that made a woman forgive us? Whatever it was, he was happy that it worked. "I love you so much," he said as he picked himself off the floor and held Rita around her waist. He continued to cry soaking her shirt with salty, phony tears.

I rubbed his head as I wondered, once again, why I kept giving in to him. I missed my old, boring peaceful life in a way. There was no drama attached to it. I was starting to see why so many beautiful women were single, but that word...."*single*"... *Did I want to go back to being single? Not really. Did I really want to give Brian another chance? Maybe. For a chance for real love, I'd probably do just about anything.*

Chapter 13

"*P*lease, come in," said Sophie as she gave Brian a quick look-over. He was even finer than the evening she'd seen him at the club. "So, did you bring your artwork?"

Brian walked right up to Sophie. He was so close to her that she could detect a hint of an Altoid on his breath. "Of course I did. That's why I'm here, right?"

Sophie liked his boldness. She decided to match it. Without any words spoken, she slowly unbuttoned his shirt, revealing a perfect masculine chest.

Brian closed his eyes and dropped the painting, purchased at Walmart for $29.95, flat on the Persian carpet. He loved when a woman took control. He let her continue her process of removing his clothing and couldn't wait to experience what she had going on in the bedroom. She was already gorgeous and rich, but a queen in the bedroom was also one of Brian's qualifications in a lover.

Sophie was nervous. She didn't know why she was doing what she was doing but she supposed that this was the same way Ahmad's women got him to cheat on her. It was her turn to be the other woman for she was tired of being the innocent victim. She lowered her body so that she could taste him. She licked, sucked and teased with her tongue. He was delicious.

Brian was in heaven or at least close to it as Sophie gave him one of the best oral sessions of his life. "Right there," he mumbled. "Yes, just like that. Oooooooooooooooh yeah!"

Sophie finished her award-winning blow job and was happy to see that Brian enjoyed it, and that pleased her even more. She excused herself to go to the bathroom to wash up and to slip into something more comfortable than the skimpy lingerie she had on for Brian's arrival. When she walked back into the living room, Brian was still naked and standing in the same position as if awaiting another pleasurable blow job. "So, ready to show me more of your artwork?" she asked.

"First, I have to see your artwork," he teased.

"Sure thing," she said as she untied her robe, revealing nothing but her birthday suit.

Chapter 14

Fatigue was starting to kick in as I went over the financial statements of Soul Expressions.

I didn't know if I was physically tired or mentally drained from Brian. Since the trip last month, there had not been any physical abuse from Brian, mainly because I gave in to his every word and that caused my stress level to shoot through the roof. It was like I was afraid of saying "no" to him.

I did not accept his marriage proposal yet, which Brian did not seem to mind. I told him that I wanted to wait until he successfully started his business.

I decided to get to the club a little earlier to find it in my budget to loan him fifty thousand dollars to start his construction business. Brian told me that he tried several banks, and no bank would fund his idea. I wasn't surprised. He couldn't possibly think he could walk into a bank with no collateral and obtain a loan for fifty grand, did he? About an hour into reviewing the financials, I realized that I would be making a terrible mistake of giving Brian the loan. That would mean cutting a few salaries, which would mean a layoff and there was no way I would do that.

Since being with Brian, my finances were melting away. I spent more on him than I thought I had. I decided against giving him the money, of course, but what I was afraid of was breaking the news to him. This would be the first disagreement since our return from Florida. I would find the courage to tell him over a romantic dinner tonight.

Since it was Wednesday, I knew the club wouldn't be too packed so I decided to head on home. My manager, Charles, could easily handle things. Charles was the only manager that I could truly put my trust in. I had not one worry if I ever had to be absent from the club; he took care of everything. Of course, I still had to be around, just in case of an emergency. It was, after all, my prized business.

I walked to the office to say goodbye to Charles, and the look on his face insinuated that he noticed the bruises on my face. Damn, I knew I should have stuck to wearing that makeup! I decided not to wear any foundation today because I felt the bruises were hardly visible anymore. Damn!

"What happened to you, girlie!" he said. "You tripped over that sad, long face of yours or something?"

"Ha ha ha, very funny, Charles. No…actually, I…um…had an accident at the airport last month. I fell over a… wet floor sign….and tripped. Hit my head on somebody's luggage. Can you believe that?"

"Yeah, sure," he said while giving me a suspicious look. "Is everything okay with you and Brian?"

I rolled my eyes at Charles. "Everything is fine with me and Brian, thank you very much," I said defensively.

"I didn't mean anything by that, Rita."

"I know." I was getting ready to walk out of the door when Charles stopped me.

"Rita!"

"Yes?"

"If there was something going on with you, you would tell me right?"

Damn, he knew! I made it so obvious. I tried to play it off. Charles was the last person I wanted in my business. "Of course, I would partner. You know me, I always have the control remember," I said as I tried to laugh off my statement. Just then, my emotions took over and my laughter turned into a desperate cry, something I tried to hold in since the day I returned from my trip from hell.

"Rita! What is going on with you?" Did Brian do this to you? That mother…"

"No!" I interrupted. I'm just having a difficult time with everything else in my life. Brian and I are just fine! Just fine!"

"Yeah, right, Rita. Whatever you say. But I'm telling you right now, if I find out that he did this to you, it's on!"

"Charles, everything is fine. Brian is fine, I am fine, my relationship is fine! Now please, don't make this into something ugly."

"Rita, all I know is that you cannot get a black eye and a lump on your head by falling into some luggage. What were they carrying in there…a sack of rocks? Now, get over here and sit! I want to talk to you!"

"No! Charles, I can't do this right now, okay?"

"Yes you can! And you need to listen to me right now!"

Damn! I guess I didn't have a choice. Charles was very concerned. I sat down with the quickness.

Charles continued on. "Any man who does this to you is not worthy of having you! Now, I won't get into your business, but I love you as a sister and as a friend. I'm going to tell you right now that if he did this to you, you need to get rid of him. There is no sense in trying to make things seem all peaches and cream. You're not fooling anyone but yourself."

"But, Charles! It's not like…"

"Let me finish, Rita. Back when I was married to Bernice, there were times when I lost my temper as well, and, well…you know the rest." Charles was on the verge of tears. "But you know what, I'm glad she left me; otherwise, I would have never known what my problem was. If we had continued our marriage, somebody would have killed somebody. But I got help, Rita. If she would take me back today, then we'd be the happiest couple in the world because now I know better. So what I'm telling you is… it is not going to go away overnight. He will continue to do this to you until one of you is dead. It took me years to come to my senses and realize that I had a problem, but it took for *me* to want to get help. And unless *he* is really ready, then it won't work. You have to leave him, Rita. Are you listening to me?"

"Yes, Charles, I'm listening," I said as I sobbed into a paper napkin. I thought I knew everything about him, but this was a shocker. Charles was the sweetest man in the world.

I pondered on what he said. "But Brian said that he was ready to get help!" I cried.

Charles snapped. "I knew it! Rita, why were you trying to cover for him? That asshole! I'm going to…"

"Calm down, Charles. Now it's my turn to talk," I cried. "Brian loves me and I love him. And I want to help him. We made an appointment for this coming weekend to see a therapist in the downtown area. Now let me do this, okay? And if it works, then fine, but on the other hand, if it doesn't work, then I'll leave him, I promise."

"Rita, honey, is Brian really ready for this?"

"Yes, Charles, yes. He told me he was ready; he told me he wanted to get help. We are going to be just fine, okay? Don't worry so much."

Charles could not believe that the woman standing before him that he'd known for ten years, as strong as she was, was backing down to a man whom he and everybody else knew was using her. He never wanted to say anything to her because she was a grown woman and knew what she was doing – or at least he hoped. "Well, Rita, like I said, I'm here for you if you need me. Whatever you need, please don't hesitate to come to me. If you want me to kick his ass, then…"

"No, no, no, Charles! That won't be necessary. We will get through this. Just trust me on this, okay?"

"Rita, if you don't mind my asking…this is not the first time you have been through a relationship like this one. Why are you doing this to yourself again?"

I was dumbfounded. I didn't have an answer to that. He made a good point. Why would I allow myself to go through another abusive relationship? "I don't know, Charles. I guess for the sake of love." That was my only realistic explanation and I was going to stick with it. Yeah, that's why. For the sake of love!

"Rita, there is no love in a fist on your face. My advise is for you to leave him. And if you don't, he'll kill you. I'm just going to be straight up with you. He will kill you! Leave him!" And with that said, Charles got up and walked to the main lobby of the club.

I thought on and on about what Charles said. Would Brian really kill me, or will we live happily ever after? I wanted to take a chance to try to make our relationship work. He hadn't raised one hand to me in a month so that meant, in my opinion, that he was trying to make this work. It doesn't matter that he canceled the last two sessions with the therapist. He promised me he would go this weekend.

I left the club with confidence in my relationship. I decided to cook smothered chicken and rice for our candlelight dinner. It was Brian's favorite and hopefully, will make it easier on me when I break the news to him of my not being able to loan him the money. That will be the real test of our love and whether or not he really wants to change. If he gets pissed off at this news, then I can finally, finally, finally get it in my head that it was never about our love – it was always about my money.

* * * *

Chapter 15

Once I arrived at my house, I saw that Brian's car was not in the driveway. Usually, he would be home around this time, but I supposed that since he was not home yet, I would have time to set up the romantic atmosphere. I decided to take a hot shower before preparing the meal. I pressed the 'play' button on my answering machine and stepped into the shower to listen to my messages. I already knew who it was. I was my posse, Jackie and Tish, wondering what in the world happened to me. They had left several messages in the past couple of months, but I've been so busy with my new man and business, that you can say I kicked them to the curb.

"First message....beep... hey girl, it's Jackie. Where have you been? I haven't heard from you in a while. Me and Tish were starting to get worried until she told me that you had a new

man! Girl, you don't have to diss us cuz you got a man now! Give me a call. Miss you!"

Beep!

"Next message... beep... hey, Ms. Poetry. I know Jackie just called cuz she can't hold water. Yes, I told her about your new man. I couldn't help it. But it's been so long for you girl! When are we going to meet this brother? You have been hiding him for five months! I saw you two going in the club the other night. Girl, he is superfine! Where'd you find that one? Anyway, sorry I couldn't stop in, I was on my way to work! Call me. Let's do lunch. Smooches!"

Beep!

"Last message... beep... This is a message for Brian. Hello, baby, its Sophie. I tried reaching you on your cell phone but couldn't get through. I just wanted to say thanks again for a wonderful evening. Call me later. Bye, Brian."

I could not believe my ears! How in the world did that tramp get my telephone number? I raced out of the shower to check the caller id. Sophie had a lot of nerves calling my house, and, to make matters worse, the heifer didn't even bother to block the call. I don't know what got into me, but I picked up the telephone and redialed the number displayed on the caller id. Just as Sophie picked up the phone, Brian walked in the door.

"Hey babe!" he said as he walked in smiling.

I was going to hang up but, fuck that, I didn't care if Brian was standing behind me, I was going to tell this woman off once and for all. "Sophie, this is Rita. How in the hell did you get *my* telephone number?"

Brian stopped in his tracks. "Rita!..."

I put up one finger to stifle him and continued to yell at Sophie. "I said, how did you get my telephone number!" I screamed into the receiver. "And why are you calling my man? Who do you think you are!"

Sophie laughed in my ear, pissing me off even more.

"Oh, girlfriend," said Sophie. "If he were your man, then he wouldn't have been with me today? By the way, when you make love to him tonight, please ask him to shower. He probably still has my smell on him," she said.

That skeezer had the nerve to hang up in my face after that skeezer-fied comment. I was furious and found myself on the verge of another panic attack. This was it and I wasn't playing this time. I had had enough; enough of him using me; enough of his cheating; enough of the whole relationship, period. When I turned around to face Brian, he was still standing there with that goofy look on his face.

"So, did you have a great time tonight?" I asked.

Brian tried to answer, but choked. "I....I.....," he stammered.

"I asked you a question, Brian. Did you have a good time tonight?"

"I don't know what you're talking about," he said as he tried to storm past me." His eyes were diverting back and forth, a sign of his being caught red-handed.

"Brian, you know what, this is it! It's over!"

"What are you talking about! You are going to take what that woman says over my word?"

"I'm not stupid, Brian. How in the world did she get my telephone number?"

" I don't know, Rita, but I'll call her back right now and ask her. She is crazy! Absolutely crazy!"

I walked up to him and sniffed his clothing. The smell of Talisman perfume almost suffocated me. "Wow, what lovely perfume? So tell me, what excuse are you going to use this time?"

"I don't know what you're talking about. I'm going to call her right now! I can't believe you! You know there's nothing going on! I already told you, that woman is after me. She's not normal, Rita. I'll call her and prove it to you. Look, I'll even put it on speakerphone."

At that moment, I had to laugh at myself. The more that I looked at that fine, gorgeous specimen before me, the more I realized that I wasn't whipped at all. I was infatuated with his looks. This man before me was nothing more than a lying gigolo. I blocked the telephone from him.

"That won't be necessary, Brian. You know, I've been thinking about us over and over again. And the truth is, I can't take – no, I won't take anymore of your shit! I want you out of my house now. And if you try anything, I will call the police!"

Brian looked frightened all of a sudden. Yep, this man was definitely hiding something from me.

"Why do you have to get the police involved? You are going to listen to her and not believe your man?"

"Brian, you are no longer my man! I don't know what I was thinking! You were just using me, weren't you? I know, stupid question. Of course you were. Well, not anymore, baby boy. Go and get your new woman to take care of you!"

I felt brave, and got in his face. The anger I felt gave me all the courage in the world.

At that moment, Brian raised his hand to slap me. I just stood there waiting. "Go ahead. Hit me, you bastard! Hit me!"

Brian just stood there with his hand in the air. I guess that was suppose to scare me, but NOT!

I stepped even closer to him. "Like I said, if you don't get the hell out of here, I will call the police! Get out!"

Brian sucked in his bottom lip and gave me a look I'll never forget. It was the kind of look that a kid would give his mother if she refused to buy him ice cream. I found it humorous though, but held in my laughter. I wasn't scared of him, but I wasn't stupid either -- well, I won't be stupid anymore.

"Fine, I'll leave, but once I'm gone, don't even bother calling me, and I will never call you again. You will never see me again."

So he wanted to play the guilt game? I wasn't falling for that either. "Fine, Brian. That's how I want it. Now, please, get your shit and get out of my house. I do not need you!" At that moment, I realized that I was being too nice. "Oh, what am I saying?" I started to laugh.

Brian laughed with me. He must have thought that I was changing my mind about kicking him out. I did the crazy woman move. One second I was laughing and the next second, I just stopped. Brian continued to laugh until he noticed that I was no longer.

"So...baby. You alright now? Is everything cool?" he asked.

Did he think it was that easy? "No, Brian. What I meant was that everything you have is what I bought you so that means that you don't have shit to take with you. You didn't think I was giving you the car, the jewelry and clothes, did you?"

Brian's smile faded. "You can't do that! You bought those things for me!"

"No, I loaned them to your broke ass."

"Rita, baby, come on. Do you know what you're doing? Do you really want to let all of this go?" he asked desperately.

"I guess you must be deaf. I don't want you! Get out!"

"Fine, Rita. That's cool. I'm outta here. But first, what about the fifty grand?"

"Negro! Do you actually think I'm that fucking stupid? I know you don't have the audacity to ask for money when I'm breaking up with you!"

"But you said…"

"Brian, please! I have given you enough. So I guess this was all about the money!"

"No, Rita, I love you!"

"You never loved me! You only used me! I was just too blind to see that! If you want to talk about love, then talk about it with Sophie! Now, get out!"

Brian walked towards the door with his head hung low.

There was one more thing. "Brian, wait!" I screamed.

He turned around revealing the sad kid look again.

I stared at him for a few seconds before speaking and then held out my hand. "My keys, please!"

That made Brian angry. He charged towards me, but stopped when I gave him an "*I dare you*" look while placing my hand on the telephone.

Spittle flew from his mouth as he yelled at me. "Who in the hell do you think you are? Oh, so now all of a sudden, you're all big and bad and bold as shit? I'll slap…"

"No, Brian, you won't slap anything," I interrupted. You remember when you hit me last month? Well, underneath this makeup, the bruises are still there and I say that these are worth at least a year in jail. And every mark you try to put on me from this point on, I will get my lawyer to persuade a jury to add a year to each additional bruise. Now go ahead, try it!"

"Fuck you, Rita!" Brian said as he threw the keys at me, barely missing my eye. He walked out of the door and hailed a cab.

I did not realize that the whole time I was standing there arguing with Brian, I didn't have a stitch of clothing on. "Well at least he got one last good look at this fabulous body."

I stepped back in the shower with a fresh feeling of relief. I still wasn't ready to go back to my lonely, single life, but anything was better than tiptoeing around my own house. At least I could finally exhale again! If only I had that same courage a month ago. *Thanks, Sophie. He's all yours now.*

* * * *

While sitting in the taxi, Brian realized that the only form of money he had on him was the credit card Rita gave him. He hoped she wouldn't notice until it was too late; he planned on going on a huge shopping spree to recover all of the items she took back, everything but the car, of course. There was only a $5,000 balance on the card and he planned on spending every last dime of it. He instructed the taxi driver to take him to his mother's house. He had to have something to drive around in and as much as he hated it, he had to retrieve his Pinto parked in his mother's garage. Boy, was he going to miss his Cadillac!

All the while, he was still angry. Not necessarily at Rita, but at Sophie. She had spoiled his chances of him finally being able to start his own business. One telephone call and his dream was ruined – just like that. He had no idea that Sophie was crazy like that. This was one of the things he hated about being a player. Sometimes a player loses his own game.

After quietly getting his car (but not too quietly for his car was louder than ever), Brian headed straight over to the home of Ms. Sophie Scott-Roberts.

* * * *

Chapter 16

"Brian, what a surprise!"

"Hello, Sophie. Can I talk to you for a minute?" Brian asked without trying to show his anger.

"Sure, come in."

Brian walked over to the lounge chair while counting back from ten. He was truly angry with her, but she was now his only chance of rising financially again and he didn't want to ruin it. He would like nothing more than to give her a piece of his mind and now, more than ever, he really did want to hit a female. "Why did you call Rita's house? Do you know what you've done? I told you, in due time, we would be together!"

"Well, you've been saying that for over a month now, and I couldn't wait any longer. I couldn't stand the fact that you were going home to another woman instead of being with me. I didn't mean to upset you; besides, you told me that you didn't love her anymore. Come on, it can't be that bad. I can offer you so much more than her anyway."

"Is that right? Well, thanks to you, Rita won't allow me to take any of my things from the house, nor would she let me get my car from her garage. I have to drive my brother's raggedly car until I can get another one," he lied.

"Why couldn't you get your car and clothing? It was yours, wasn't it?"

"The car was in both of our names, and as far as the clothing, she burned all of them. I told you she was crazy! I told you she would take it hard if she found out about us. Now, thanks to you, I don't have anything now! Why couldn't you just wait?"

"I'm sorry, Brian. I truly am."

Brian gave Sophie a questionable look. "Is that all you have to say? What am I going to do now?"

"Why don't you spend the night and in the morning, you can go over there and get what's yours. And tomorrow, I'll help you find an apartment."

"Didn't you just hear what I said, Sophie? There's nothing. She took everything from me and there is no way I can get it back!"

Sophie fiddled her hands, afraid of looking him in the eye. "Then where are you going to live?"

"I figured that since you worked so hard to break us up and succeeded, then I thought you would let me crash here with you."

"With me?"

"Yes, is that a problem? You got what you wanted, right?"

"Why are you being so rude? I didn't know that she would put you out right away. I guess I got carried away, you know?"

"You did get carried away, there's no mistaken about that! You know, that's not all though. Rita also took all of my money out of my account."

"*All* of your money? How much!"

"Fifty Thousand Dollars."

"Fifty grand? So how are you going to get it back?"

"I don't think I can. There was no proof that she stole it from me. We had a joint account."

Things weren't making sense to Sophie. He didn't seem like the kind of man that would let a woman get away with taking everything from him. Sophie realized that what she had before her was a man who had not a pot to piss in. "So, what you are saying is, you don't have any money, clothing, car, nothing?"

"That's what I'm saying. I was planning on leaving her soon and planned to get everything together before she found out about us, but you went and ruined everything." Brian held his head down low. The puppy dog look didn't work with Rita, be he hoped it would work with Sophie.

Sophie felt sorry for him. She didn't realize that she would cause this much drama to his life. "I'm so sorry. You poor baby. Well, since all of this is my fault, then I guess I can't object to your staying here. I guess it's no problem that I go out and buy you a few things until you get yourself situated."

"I would appreciate that."

"Why don't you let me call her. I'm sure that..."

"No! You've done enough! Let me handle things with her from now on. Now, I'm here with you. This is what you wanted, right?"

"Brian, this is all happening so fast. I...I don't know!"

Brian walked up to her and the anger he tried to hide came about. "What do you mean, you don't know! You got me kicked out, didn't you? Why would you want to do that and then tell me you don't know what you want!"

Sophie backed away. "You're right, Brian. I...I g...guess this is what I want. Please stop being so rude. I just wanted....I....I do want to be with you. I guess I got a little crazy, huh?"

"Crazy isn't the word for what you did!"

"Okay, okay! I apologize again. Why don't you go upstairs and take a shower. I'll put dinner on and afterwards, we can talk, okay?"

"Okay. But first, come here for a second."

"For what?" Sophie asked nervously.

"So I can give my new woman a kiss."

"Oh, okay then." She hesitated, but then decided to walk over to him. She now wondered if she made a mistake. Now that she had finally "won" him, she didn't know what to do next for she wasn't accustomed to doing what she never thought she would do – stealing another woman's man.

She kissed him and then something came over her. She realized that maybe it was all worth it for no one set her body on fire like Brian.

* * * *

Chapter 17

I'd never felt so free, yet so alone. After sitting down and thinking of all of the problems that Brian and I endured; for example, him being broke, his abuse, his lying (and oh, did I mention him being broke?), I realized that he wasn't worth another minute of my time. Yes, I laughed at myself, after the fact, for being so stupid and so vulnerable. One thing my mother taught me was to never ever spoil a man and that was exactly what I did. I promised myself never again to put myself in that type of situation again. I pulled out my notepad and wrote down my agenda for finalizing my relationship with Brian.

    (1) *report credit card stolen;*

    (2) *sell the Cadillac;*

    (3) *donate his clothing to Good Will;*

> *(4) send the jewelry as Christmas gifts to my three male cousins and one uncle; and*
>
> *(5) Get comforter dry-cleaned which smelled of Brian's cologne.*

I didn't want anything in my home to remind me of Brian. It was time to move on.

After I reported my credit card stolen, I decided to return a few telephone calls. It had been a while since I spoke to my best friend, Jackie. She was probably upset with me for not calling, but knowing her, she got over it.

Jackie answered on the first ring.

"Hello."

"Hey, Jack, what's up?"

"What's up stranger!" Jackie screamed into the receiver.

"Everything. I am super busy at the club and had a lot of drama with Brian lately. I just broke up with him."

"Really? Well, that didn't last long. I haven't even met the brother yet."

"He wasn't worth it, girl!"

Jackie detected the sorrow in my voice. "What happened? Are you okay?"

"Girl, he was an animal!"

Jackie laughed. "What do you mean…like in the bedroom?"

"No, girl! Well...yes...that too, but I'm talking about outside of the bedroom. Girl, you remember Keith, my ex, don't you?"

"Not that woman-beating bastard!" Jackie screamed. She could not stand to hear that man's name.

"Yes, that one!"

"Are you telling me that Brian hit you too?"

"Try more like beat me down and not just once!"

"And why are you just now telling me this? Why didn't you call me sooner?"

"Because I remember the last time I had you all involved. You damn near killed Keith and I just didn't need all the drama this time!"

"Oh, it's like that? I was just looking out for you! I only shot the man in the foot, I wasn't trying to kill him!"

"I know, and I appreciate you looking out for me. I'm just glad the court let you off. But I handled it and he's gone."

"He didn't give you any problems, did he?"

"No, not really. Tried to get some money out of me though."

"No, he didn't!" Jackie screamed.

"Girl, yes. I didn't tell you that he also met some woman at my club and came in yesterday from sleeping with her?"

"Really? Who?"

"Some no-good hoochie named Sophie. She kind of resembles Robin Givens."

"You're not talking about Sophie Scott-Roberts are you?"

Rita ran over to her caller id to confirm Sophie's last name. "Yes, that's her! Girl, she is a straight up bitch. She did every and anything in her power to steal Brian from me. Well, she got what she wanted. She could have him! How do you know her?"

"Girl, she was married to my friend, Ahmad, and he used to tell me all kinds of things about her, like how she would go crazy if she didn't get her way. He said the only thing that made her happy was money and weed. But her stealing your man is not like her. That's weird."

"Well she did it. And if she is crazy, then her and Brian are going to be some couple", I laughed.

Jackie suddenly didn't find it so humorous anymore. "Girl, if that's the case, then that's going to be one hell of a violent relationship. You may want to warn her of how he is."

I was shocked that those words came from my best friend's mouth. "What the hell for? She called my house disrespecting me! Whatever happens to her, shit, she deserves it!"

"Well, whatever. I'm just saying…but, anyway, I'm on my way. I know you need a shoulder to cry on right now."

"You know I do. Believe it or not, I'm a little sad. I can really use the company and I'll have your favorite drink waiting for you when you get here."

"No more Grey Goose and cranberry juice for me, I switched over to Hypnotic."

"Hyp what?"

"Hypnotic. You'll like it. I'll pick up a few bottles on my way."

"Now how is it that you hear about the new drinks before I do and I own a night club?"

"Cuz, I'z a true alcoholic, girl. See you in an hour."

"Bye girl."

Chapter 18

While I was doing my 'welcome' rounds with my customers, I spotted Brian and Sophie sitting in the middle section of the club. For some reason, I knew that I wouldn't see the last of Brian, but never in a million years did I think that he would have the nerve to show up at the poetry club.

I had to maintain my professionalism, but a small twinge of jealousy raced through me. Brian was looking better than ever and Sophie, who made sure everyone knew he was her man, couldn't keep her hands off of him. I wasn't jealous of them being together as a couple, I was jealous because I knew that Brian was rocking Sophie's world in the bedroom and that I wouldn't be getting any more of that good lovin'.

The regulars in the club all gave me quizzical looks because they were accustomed to

Brian and me sitting at the head of the stage, not him being there with another woman. I explained to a few of my customers about the breakup and figured they would spread the word for me.

I continued my rounds but decided not to go to Brian and Sophie's table, but before I headed to the stage to introduce the first poet, Sophie yelled my name so loudly that everyone in the club turned around to see who was being so ghettorific in a place so sophisticated. I put on my best imitation of a professional smile and walked over to the table. "Yes, Sophie. What can I do for you? And hello, Brian."

Brian smirked at me -- I guess to let me know that he had no problem getting another woman who could take care of him. "Hello, Rita, and how are you this...." he said before being interrupted by Sophie.

Sophie cleared her throat loud enough for everyone to glance our way again.

"This glass is terribly dirty, Rita. Is there any way I can get another drink in a *clean* glass?"

I looked around at the other patrons, hoping that they did not hear that comment, but I guess they did because they all started to inspect their glasses as if they had never had a drink in my establishment before. I was totally humiliated. "Sophie, I know what you are trying to do and it will not be necessary! You win, okay?"

Sophie reached over and massaged Brian's arm. She then directed her attention back to me.

"I win? What are you talking about? I'm not playing any games with you, Rita. Now if I take a sip out of this filthy glass and get sick, then I'm going to be winning this club in a lawsuit!"

Brian sat there as if he were enjoying the altercation between us. I knew he could be childish, but never in a million years would I have thought that he would be like this. It was like he was rooting Sophie on to continue to embarrass me.

I signaled for one of my bartenders to refill Sophie's drink and walked away with my eyes planted on the floor to the stage to introduce the first poet of the evening. I didn't want to make matters any worse with Sophie. After my conversation with Jackie the other night, I knew why Sophie behaved the way she did. Jackie told me of Sophie's ex-husband's many lovers, and I could now see how it would make one crazy in a way. I sort of felt sorry for Sophie, but after what she just pulled in my club, I didn't give a damn what happened to her.

I grabbed the microphone and pulled myself together. "Ladies and gentlemen, I apologize for the delay of the show and my rudeness this evening." I gave Sophie a *"please be on your best behavior"* stare. "But I'm going to make it up to you by bringing to the stage, the bad boy of poetry, Mr. Marcus Blackhawk!"

The crowd applauded. Marcus was somewhat of a comedic poet. There was always something in his poetry that would make people laugh. Marcus ran on the stage and grabbed the mic. "Ladies and gentlemen, tonight, I want to do something different. I've created a piece dedicated to my sister, who passed away last month. She suffered from postpartum depression and took her life." Tears rolled down his eyes. The crowd was silent for a moment and then applauded. Everyone then became silent to let Marcus pour out his emotions. Marcus began. He closed his eyes and frowned his face to let us know that this piece was truly from his heart and there was nothing funny about it.

I am drowning myself in my own self-pities
Complicating my complications in life
Death was the only thing that soothed me
So I commenced to the kitchen to fetch my knife

As I stand here wounding myself
I'm thinking of how all this began
I wanted children – oh how I prayed for them
And I was blessed with Little Lynn

Giving birth to Little Lynn only months ago
Oh! how much I adored her
Then all of a sudden my heart turned cold and I had no clue
As to what love was like anymore

As time went on I noticed my love for Little Lynn was fading
I'd reject her her feedings
and ignore her all day
And realized how I couldn't stand my own baby

And I'd also reject myself and had no feelings
And I'd sleep and sleep all day
I didn't care about cleaning myself either
I felt like such a waste

Why do I not love her anymore?
Why do I not love myself anymore?

I left Little Lynn with my mom

who loved her more than I did
And I went into town to see my physician,
this is what he said:

He told me about this postpartum syndrome
A bunch of pills I would pop
They'd work for a minute and I thought I was winning
Against this disease that made me stop

Loving Her...
Loving Myself...

I was taking medication in order to love her
My only flesh who's flesh is of my flesh
I thought motherhood would be great for me
But I was always down and depressed

She'd look at me with loving eyes longing for my attention
But I'd turn and walk away from her
Hating myself for treating Little Lynn this way
I finally came up with an answer

I remembered watching the news one night
and heard of babies being killed
Because of this disease created by Satan
innocent babies' blood was spilled

So I dropped Little Lynn off to my mom's
she will definitely be loved by her
And now here I stand at my kitchen counter
stabbing myself harder...

And Harder...
And Harder...
And Harder...

Until I felt nothing but peace within me

The crowd gave Marcus a standing ovation. Many of the audience also cried with him. I then walked onstage to comfort Marcus who was so emotionally wrapped up, he couldn't leave the stage. It was as if he felt he was leaving a part of his sister up there.

"Rita!" an annoying voice yelled from the back. "Get off the stage! Rita! I need you over here to refill my drink! Rita!"

Everyone looked to the middle section of the club to witness Sophie acting a fool! She was sitting on Brian's lap waiving her arms to get my attention. In the other hand was her empty glass. It had been obvious that she had too much to drink, but it also seemed to me that she was trying to steal the attention away from me and Marcus. Marcus then walked backstage to mourn in private.

"Rita!" Sophie screamed. "Rita! I need a drink!"

Enough was enough! I marched down from the stage and signaled for the security guard to follow. "Sophie, you are being very rude tonight, and I think that it's time for you and Brian to leave!"

"Oh, it's like that, Rita?" Brian asked.

Oh no he didn't! "Oh, now you want to speak up? Well, too late now, Brian! You know the rules of this club!"

Sophie stood and got in my face. "I will leave when my man gets his money, car and clothing! You can't keep it! It's his!"

"Sophie…let's go!" Brian yelled.

I was speechless. *Did Sophie actually believe those lies?* I looked at Brian and saw that he was suddenly very nervous. "Sophie, just so you know, he's broke. I don't have..."

"Shut up, Rita!" Brian interrupted.

The audience seemed to be more entertained by the scene with me, Brian and Sophie than with the poets. I knew I had to end the shenanigans. "Security, just escort them out and make sure that they are never allowed back in here."

Sophie screamed in my face. "You can't do that! We'll sue you! My man wants his shit back!"

I wasn't going to say anything, but Sophie was acting like she was brainwashed or something and that was when I took a good look at myself. Was I this fooled by him?

Sophie needed to hear the truth. "Sophie," I said. "Brian is lying to you...He doesn't have...."

Smack! I didn't see it coming, but the stinging pain on my face told all. Someone hit me. I didn't know whether I passed out or went into shock because when I finally came to, tables and chairs were flying all over my establishment. Sophie stood over me yelling in my face while Charles was beating the crap out of Brian. I stood only to be pushed back down again by Sophie. I wasn't sure who hit me in my face, but it didn't matter...now was the perfect moment to finally do what I'd been wanting to do for the last two weeks -- kick Sophie's ass up and down Harvey street.

Chapter 19

"Girl, what happened last night?" Jackie asked anxiously. "I heard about the brawl over at your club."

Tish walked to the wet bar and poured each of us a glass of Hypnotic, our new girlfriend drink. "Yeah, girl, I heard that you beat the shit out of Ahmad's ex-wife, but by the looks of your face, it looks a lot more like she beat the shit out of you!"

"Damn, you know Sophie too? How is it that everyone knows who this woman is, except me?" I asked. "Is she famous or something?"

Tish finished her drink in one swallow. "No, she isn't, but everyone knows Ahmad. He's that fine man who owns AMS Consulting Corporation. And very friendly, I might add. I don't see why she divorced him. Hell, I wouldn't have let that man go for anything in the world."

"Looks and money aint everything, Tish," I said.

"And you would know, wouldn't you, Ms. Give My Man Fifty Grand?"

I whipped my head at Jackie. She couldn't hold water.

Jackie choked. "Rita, she made me tell! I'm still in shock that you even offered him that kind of money. That was really not your style, hon."

I lowered my head and closed my eyes. "I don't know what I was thinking even offering it to him. I guess I thought it would put him on his feet and then we could finally grow together, you know what I mean? I had long term plans of being with him."

"Even after the fights?" Jackie asked.

"What fights!" Tish screamed.

I rolled my eyes at Jackie. "If you could tell her about the money, then you might as well told her about the fights."

Tish was shocked. "You and Brian fought? You mean, "put em' up" kind of fights?"

"Yeah."

"And you had long term plans of being with him? Girl, are you out of your mind? You remember your last relationship! I know you're not that hard up for a man that you would go through that shit again!"

I sighed. "I guess I was. I spend so much time at the club that I don't get to go out often and meet decent men."

Jackie and Tish both asked their question at the same time. "Where did you meet Brian?"

All of us bursted out in laughter.

"Jinks," said Tish.

"I met him online," I said as I quickly looked away from my friends.

Suddenly, everyone was silent. I knew that I should have withheld that information.

Again, in unison, "ON-LINE!"

"Yes, online! I read an article in Essence that stated that women meet good men online all the time."

"It also said in Essence that if you use the George Foreman Lean, Mean Fat Burning Grilling Machine, then you'll lose a lot of weight! Shit, I aint lost a pound!" said Tish.

"Tish, you don't have the good sense God gave you, you know that?" Jackie said while cracking up.

"I'm serious," said Tish. "You can't get all your life's lessons in a magazine. And I hope you learned your lesson, girlfriend. You met an online psycho, he uses you for your money, fights you, and now sends his new girlfriend to kick your ass? What kind of shit is that? If that's your idea of a good man, then you're right, you don't get out much!"

I was shamed. My girlfriends were not making me feel any better. I heard of women meeting crazy men online, but I figured it wouldn't happen to me. "Yes, he was crazy, I do admit that," I said. "But for the record, Sophie didn't lay one hand on me. Apparently, it was Brian who hit me to keep me from telling her the truth about him."

Jackie looked as if she wanted to cry. "Brian was the one who hit you at the club?"

"Yeah, and it was a good thing Charles was around. He came to my rescue and gave Brian a taste of his own medicine."

Tish poured herself another glass and refilled mine. I was guzzling down the blue liquor.

"So, what happened after that?" Jackie asked.

I took another huge swallow of my drink before telling the rest of the details. "Well, while Charles was beating the living daylights out of Brian, and after Sophie pushed me back down on the floor, I got back up and punched her in her face because I figured it was her who hit me in the first place. Well after I punched her, she told me that she pushed me down because a chair almost hit me in the head. And then she started to cry. At first I thought I punched her too hard because she was really crying – like a 2 year old who couldn't get a lollipop. She started babbling all of these apologies to me. I didn't understand until now. She was apologizing to me because of the way

Brian knocked me out in front of her. I guess she got scared or something."

Jackie interrupted. "You *guess* she got scared! She probably looked at him in a totally different light after seeing that!"

Tish smacked her lips loud enough for the world to hear. "Will you hush up and let her finish?"

"Who you telling to hush?"

"You, Boo Boo! Let the girl finish!"

"Whatever Scrappy Doo!" Jackie rolled her eyes at Tish and directed me to continue.

"Before I finish, let me just tell you two that yall are really special, and I don't mean that in a good way!" I said.

"Whatever!" said Tish.

Jackie's buzz was starting to take effect. She thought my comment was hilarious and started cracking up. "Gone ahead and finish, girl."

"Anyway", I continued. "She started acting all crazy and telling me that he made her act that way at the club. Like telling her what to say about the glass being dirty and everything. She said that the only reason she did it was because he said that I wouldn't give him his money and car. But before I could say anything back to her, guess who pulls her by the arm and drags her all the way to the car?"

"Brian!" they both said.

"Girl, his face was full of blood too. Almost didn't recognize him. Charles really did a number on him. I felt sorry for Sophie though. She looked terrified on her way out."

"Serves that witch right. That's what she get for letting a man tell her when and where to act ghetto," said Tish. "By the way, what money and car is she talking about?"

Damn, I wanted to slap myself for saying too much. "Well, you already know about the fifty grand I was going to give him. Well, apparently, he lied to her about me taking it from him, like it was his in the first place. But what I didn't tell you was that I bought him a Cadillac....It's in the garage."

Tish and Jackie damn near fell out! "You what!" Tish screamed.

Jackie was speechless. All she could do was shake her head back and forth slowly.

"I know. That was dumb too, right? Go ahead. Let it all out. Feel free to call me all the names in your minds right now."

"Oh, you don't want to know the names I have for you right now, girl!" Jackie screamed. "Dummy, Stupid, Whipped, Gigolo Lover, Desperate! Oops, sorry, did I say those out loud?"

"Was the dick that dickalicious?" asked Tish. "Damn, what was it about him that made you do all of those things? I saw him and yes, he was fine, but damn, not fine enough to buy a Cadillac for. Girl, are you sure you weren't abducted by aliens and they switched you and some desperate chick's minds? What in the ...!"

"Okay! Okay! Let it go. It's over and done with now. I was stupid, okay?" I said.

"Stupid, Whipped, Desperate..."

"Jackie, that's enough!" I screamed. Damn, they had me feeling really bad!

"Sorry girl," said Jackie. "But seriously, what were you thinking? I have never known you to do such things. You were the one telling us that you will never loan a brotha a penny if he asked for it."

I was embarrassed and I knew my friends were telling me the truth. "Yeah, but it's easier said than done. I've never been with anyone who was broke so I didn't know how bad it would really be. Yes he was broke, but I thought he had potential. Not to mention that he was fine as hell. I guess I was trying to hold on to a fantasy. Shame on me, right?"

"Shame on you and shame on him for using you like that. That brother wasn't nothing nice," said Tish.

"Yeah, I know," I said. But he was something nice to look at. He started off real smooth, you know? Kind of brainwashed me."

"Kind of?" said Tish as she refilled her glass.

"Okay, he did brainwash me. And now he's going to brainwash her. Oh, well, she deserves everything that man puts her through. That's what the hell she gets."

Jackie looked at her friend. "You're not right for saying that. No one deserves to get beat on by any man."

"Well, I look at it like this, Jackie. She called my house and was throwing her and Brian's affair all in my face. She disrespected me. She comes to my club and acts a damn fool. All of my customers had to see that mess. I have to close the club for a few days for repair, so now, I'm out of a lot of money. What she did was uncalled for and now she will pay."

"Again," said Jackie. "You're not right for that, but I kind of know how you feel. But didn't you say that she apologized to you after the fight?"

"It's a little too late for apologies now," I said. You see this bruise on my face? Well, I had a few before this one and now she will know the true meaning of fighting for what you want!"

"Are you going to press charges against them?" asked Tish.

"No, I don't have time to be in court with everything I have to do at the club. Charles and I banned them from entering the club, and I am going to hire off-duty police officers to assist in security. I should be fine."

Jackie kicked off her shoes and let the buzz take its effect in her mind. "But the real question is, is Sophie going to be fine?"

"Who cares?" I said.

Jackie gave me a disappointed look. "You should care. I mean, I feel sorry for her knowing what he will probably do to her. And when something happens, aren't you going to feel kind of guilty?"

"Hell no!" I screamed. "Who's side are you on?"

"Look, Rita. We have been friends since way back. But I also used to hang with Sophie when she was with Ahmad. She's not a bad person, Rita. She's just going through a lot of changes because of the way Ahmad did her. We've all been there."

"Rita, Jackie has a point," said Tish.

"Well, I'll think about it. Right now, I have other things to concentrate on," I said.

We continued on drinking until we all passed out. I didn't give second thought to what Jackie and Tish were trying to tell me. I truly didn't give a damn about what happened to Sophie and probably never will.

* * *

Chapter 20

"Why did you hit her like that!" Sophie screamed. Brian had never answered her question from the other night. He changed the subject every time. This time, Sophie demanded an answer.

"Baby, I love you, but what happened between me and Rita is none of your concern," he said.

"None of my concern? Do you actually think that I'm not to be concerned as to why you hit that woman?"

"I hit her because I thought that she was going to attack you! Are you happy now?"

"No! I'm not happy about that. She was trying to tell me something. What are you trying to hide from me?"

"I'm not trying to hide anything. If she was going to tell you anything, it would be nothing but a bunch of lies anyway."

"How do you know it would be lies? How do you know that she wasn't offering your stuff back?"

Something was not right about the other night. Sophie was starting to become very suspicious of Brian. Rita was trying to tell her something and she had to know what that something was. The way Brian hit Rita like she were a man showed her that it may not have been her who broke them up, but a hidden secret that only Rita and Brian knew of.

Brian sat next to Sophie on the loveseat, grabbed both of her hands and placed them over his heart. "Baby, let's get one thing straight. Rita is not the kind of woman who would return my belongings to me. She was a money hungry woman, a golddigger. That's why it wasn't hard to walk away from her when she put me out. I've been trying to get out of that relationship for a while, but she always threatened that I would regret it if I did. I was scared of her in a way – not knowing what she would do next. Let's forget about Rita. I can start over and come up again, but I'm going to need your help."

"What do you mean?" Sophie asked. "Are you going to start working on some of your paintings, because I have never seen you paint anything! What ever happened with that?"

Brian had totally forgotten about that lie. He threw Sophie's hands out of his and stood up.

"Well...about that... well, see...that art dealer in Florida I told you about? They denied me a deal... and um, I figured that I would try and do something else with my life, like start my own construction business or something."

"I didn't know you were into construction. Is that what you were doing before the art?" Sophie already knew his answer and she knew it would be a lie. After she saw that "so-called" painting of what Brian brought over on their first date, she knew that he had not painted the work himself. Her mother had that same exact painting locked in her attic.

"Yes, I worked at a construction company, but I quit. See, I want my own company. I don't want to work for anyone anymore."

"I see." Sophie knew what was coming next. She braced herself for the big question.

"I want to know that, since Rita won't return my money, if it would be possible for you to loan me some money so that I can get my business started."

Sophie wanted to laugh. She had always had men who took care of her. Never in a million years did she think that she would be the one to be used. "I'm sorry, Brian, but I can't do that. All of my money is tied up in stocks and bonds and I only have enough to support myself right now," she lied.

Brian looked stunned. *She messed me up with Rita, and now doesn't want to help me out? Who does she think she's messing with?* "Sophie, I see the way you're living, and I know you got plenty of money. So, what is the real reason you don't want to help me out? I mean, you caused all of this. I just don't understand."

Sophie could not believe the words that dared to come out of Brian's mouth. Her money was her money and that was that. She had already purchased a whole new wardrobe for him and let him drive one of her cars, but that was as far as she would go. She found one of Rita's credit cards in Brian's pant pocket, but she didn't understand why he would have it, until now. Now, it was all coming to her. She vowed after the shopping spree, that she would not spend another penny on him.

He tried to make her feel guilty just about everyday they were together. Those little comments he made from time to time would actually make her feel guilty, but she would be damned if he was going to continue to do that to her. *Well, you wanted this, right baby? Until I get my things back, you are going to have to help me, bla bla bla.* Those comments were really starting to piss her off.

Yes, she did steal Brian from Rita. Yes, she thought she wanted him. But now she didn't care if he left and went back to her. There was no way in hell that she would be with a man like him who had absolutely no job, no benefits, and absolutely no shame of hitting women.

She thought long and hard before commenting on Brian's accusation of her ruining his life. "Brian, if you really wanted your things back from Rita, there are a lot of ways you can get them back. I can direct you to a lawyer. But you are not going to sit here and try to make me feel so guilty that I would cough up a penny just so you can go and get a business started. If you wanted to start a business, there are several banks in the neighborhood and Sophie International Bank is now closed! Now I know I may have caused the breakup with you and Rita, and I'm sorry. But this is not going to work out between you and I. Now, if you'll excuse me. I'll leave you to gather your things. You can take all of the clothes I bought you and your keys to that piece of junk in my garage is in the top drawer in the kitchen." Sophie got up from the loveseat and headed towards the kitchen to retrieve Brian's keys to the Pinto.

Brian's thoughts went a mile a minute. *Who does this woman think she is! So she thinks that she can get rid of me just like that? She thinks that I am just suppose to leave like a little puppy? This shit is not going to happen – not again!*

Brian ran into the kitchen and grabbed Sophie by her hair. Sophie screamed as she grabbed a frying pan on the isle of the stove. She tried to swing it hard at him but it slipped from her hand. She saw the rage in Brian's eyes. He looked as if he transformed into a monster and that look terrified her. "Stop! Let me go, you son of a bitch!" she screamed.

Brian laughed the laugh of a deranged man. "You think you're funny, don't you? You think you can put me out after all of the mess you caused in my life? Well, think again, bitch!" Brian threw Sophie over the kitchen table and then walked over to her. He lowered himself on his knees to look at her face to face. "Let me tell you something," he said with spittle seeping from the corner of his mouth, "I'm not going anywhere! And I'm going to tell you something else! You try to get rid of me, and I'll make sure you wished you never met me in the first place! And if I find out that you told anyone about this, then, well, you know...." Brian laughed again.

Just then the telephone rang. Sophie and Brian both looked at the telephone. "Go ahead and answer it," Brian said. "And make sure you remember what I just said."

Every bone in Sophie's body ached as she retreated from the floor. She tried to steady her trembling hands when she picked up the telephone. "Hel...hello."

"Hey baby. What's going on?" Paulette said. "I haven't heard from you in a while. "Is everything okay?"

"Oh...I'm...fine...mother," Sophie said while trying to remain calm.

"Are you sure, baby?"

"Yeah, ma. Look, can I call you back?"

Paulette had never heard her daughter sound so frightened and that scared her. "Baby, I'm on my way over..."

"No!" Sophie screamed. "I mean...no....mother, you don't have to come over here. I'm fine, I promise. Just feeling a little sick though. I may be coming down with some kind of flu."

"Baby, I know you've been seeing that Brian guy. Is he there with you now?"

"No, mother, he's not here. And who told you that? I'm not seeing anyone."

"Brian told me when I called the other day. Since when did you start lying to me?"

"Ma, I'll call you back, okay? I love you." Sophie hung up the telephone and slowly looked over at Brian.

Brian pouted his lips. "Are you mad at me?" he said sympathetically, then bursting out into another horrible laughter.

"You are crazy!" Sophie screamed.

"Yeah, you may be right. But the truth is, I'm just tired of being put out on my ass by you so called "strong black women". Like you, for example. You try everything in your power to take me away from a situation that I was very comfortable with. And eventually, you win. And now, you kick me out just because I'm not up to your standards. That shit is just not fair. And I'm not going to stand for it anymore."

"So, what are you thinking? That I'm going to take care of you?" Sophie asked as the tears poured from her eyes.

"Yep, that's exactly what you are going to do!" Brian screamed. He paced up and down the kitchen floor and grabbed both sides of his temple. He stopped pacing, took a deep breath, walked over to Sophie and kissed her on her forehead. He then left the kitchen and headed towards the bedroom.

Sophie felt as if she were dreaming. Can this really be happening to her? She walked over to the counter to grab her keys to head out to her mother's house. She had to get out of there. She tried to disarm the alarm, but was so nervous that she entered the wrong password. Her hands were shaking so badly that she dropped the keys, as well. She entered the password again and succeeded, but when she reached down to grab her keys, she saw two feet marching towards her.

"Where are you going?" Brian asked.

"I was going to see my mother," Sophie said nervously.

"Why?"

"Do I need a reason to see my own mother?" Sophie refused to back down to Brian. She would be no one's victim.

"You do now. And since you don't have good reason, then come and take a nap with me. I need a soft body next to me right now."

"Brian, I'm going to my mother's house! You think you can keep me locked in here with you? I don't think so! And I'm serious about you getting out of here! You think that you're going to hold me hostage in my own house? Is this how you treated Rita?"

"The way I treated Rita is none of your business! And I'm not going anywhere! I'm staying right here! So, go to your mother's house if you want. Your mother…Paulette, right? She's such a beautiful woman. I would hate for anything to happen to her, you know?"

"What is that suppose to mean?"

"It means whatever you think it means! You go to your mother's house, but if you think you're going to go over there telling her what just happened, then you are going to regret it big time."

"You wouldn't!"

"Oh, yes, I would. Now go tell mom I said hello, and give her a kiss for me."

Sophie was furious, yet frightened by his threat to hurt her mother. What did she get herself into? She stormed out of her house, got in her car and sped off. She decided against going to her mother's house, she had to talk to Rita – asap!

* * * *

Chapter 21

"What are *you* doing here?" Never in a million years would I have thought that Sophie would be standing on my doorstep. She looked horrible. The bruises on her face told all; Brian beat her.

"Rita, I need to talk to you, please. It's Brian. He's...."

I interrupted Sophie, already knowing what she was going to say. "He hit you, didn't he? Well, why are you telling me? Don't you have a telephone? I believe the number is 9-1-1."

"Rita, I can't go to the police until I speak with you first. Please. I need your help."

"Sophie, there is nothing that we need to talk about."

"But..."

"But, nothing! You got what you wanted! Hope you're happy now!" I could no longer look at her so I slammed the door in her face.

Sophie apparently didn't get the hint. She screamed through my front door.

"Rita, he's threatened to hurt my mother if I called the police! I need your help! I need any information you could give me on him so that I can get out of this safely! I need to know if he's as dangerous as I think he is and if he would really harm my mother if I were to go to the police. Help me, Rita. Please!" she cried.

I could not believe this woman was standing here begging for my help. "Sophie, I can't help you! Please get away from my door or I'll call the police on you!"

"Rita, please! I'm sorry about that night at the club and the phone calls. Please let me talk to you! My mother may be in danger! It's not just about me anymore! Brian has flipped out on me! I can't go to the police! Please!"

I wondered whether Brian was violent enough to actually do harm to Sophie's mother, and after reminiscing on the times that he beat me, I felt that there was a strong possibility that he would. Feeling bad, I almost opened the door to let her in, but flashes of Sophie embarrassing me at the club continued to invade my mind. I changed my mind. "Sophie, I can't help you! Sorry! Please leave!"

My pride wouldn't allow me to help her out. I knew what Sophie was dealing with, but there was nothing I could do for her anyway. Besides, I didn't want to go backwards, I had to continue forth with my life without Brian and all of his madness.

* * * *

Sophie felt so alone. Rita was right for not wanting to help her. She had no one to turn to – not one friend. If she told her mother of the fight and the threat that Brian made, Sophie was afraid that he would actually follow through with his threat. Her mother was all she had. Sophie's brother, Carl, had been a sergeant in the military and she hadn't spoken with him in years. If only he were here to protect her like a big brother should. All of her "so called" friends stopped calling her. She had no one to turn to. If only Rita would talk to her – give her any information about Brian so that she would know what actions to take. Sophie looked down at her feet and tried one last attempt at trying to talk to Rita. She rang the doorbell once more. "Rita, I promise you, if you would just help me, I'll pay for all the damages at your club! I'll make it up to you! I'm so sorry! Please, please let me talk to you!" she cried.

The last comment Rita yelled through the door, hurt Sophie more than Brian's fist: *"By the way Sophie, thank you for taking him off my hands!"* The only other thing Sophie heard was Rita's stereo blasting in the background – a sign that it was time for her to leave.

Chapter 22

"Instead of Sophie heading back home, she decided to make a quick stop to her dealer's house and purchase a small sack of weed to calm her nerves. She'd quit just a month ago and now she was feeling disappointed in herself because she was going back to it again. But she needed a stress reliever. She couldn't believe that she allowed herself to get into this type of situation. Why did it have to backfire on her? Why did Ahmad have to cheat on her? Why couldn't her life just go back to the way it was? Why did she even think of stealing another woman's man just because someone stole hers? Her mother had been right all along. She should have left Brian alone from the start. But now it was too late. She was trapped in her own home with a monster – a monster with no job, no money and quick hands.

Sophie rang the doorbell of Tyrone's house and was surprised to see that he was home. "What's going on, Tyrone? You got any merchandise for me today?"

Tyrone was shocked to see Sophie. He hadn't seen her in weeks and was usually the one who dropped off the package to Sophie's house. "Why didn't you just call me? What's up with you popping up here? You aint never did that before," he said while looking suspiciously at Sophie.

"I know," said Sophie. "I was in the neighborhood and realized that I need a joint to calm my nerves. Don't worry, this is not a setup, and I am not wearing a wire, okay?"

"You must be under some serious stress popping up here unannounced. Damn, what happened to you? You get mugged out here or something?"

"No….look, can I just..?"

Tyrone saw that he was embarrassing Sophie. "Well, you need to get that eye checked out….Anyway, you're lucky you were one of my best customers or I'll have to check you. What are you looking for – some weed?" he asked.

"Yeah, just about $100 worth. That should last me about another month or so. You got any?" she asked.

"Nope. I'm all out. I'm not selling weed anymore. I've moved on to the real deal." Tyrone dug into his pants pockets and pulled out a few small bags which contained a product that looked like a small white rock.

"What is that?" Sophie asked.

"This is what we call the real deal. It's crack cocaine, but this aint your average crack, this shit here is straight from Columbia. This is the real shit."

"No, thank you," Sophie said. "Who can I get my weed from then if you're not selling it?"

"I don't know. Nobody around here though – I can tell you that. When this shit right here hit the neighborhood, everybody who sell weed dropped out and started handling this shit right here."

"What am I going to do?" Sophie asked. "I need something to clear my head tonight."

"Why don't you just try one of these. It aint going to hurt you and you won't get hooked on it or nothing after just one time. Believe me, this shit right here would clear your head faster than any joint could. After you hit this shit, you'll be straight, believe that."

Sophie looked into her dealer's face and saw that he was serious about what he asked of her. "And how do you know? You've tried it?"

"Of course, I did. I test out everything I sell, just to make sure the shit is tight. And this right here is da bomb!"

Sophie never thought in a million years that she would want to get any higher than weed could take her, but with the situation going on at home, she needed something at that moment. "Okay, I'll try one, but you have to show me how to do it," she said regretfully.

"Are you sure?" Tyrone asked. He'd been knowing Sophie for years and knew that once you took one hit off the pipe, that there was no turning back. But money was money and he knew that Sophie would become another one of his high-paying customers. He knew she was rich, and if he could stop smoking more than he was actually selling, he would be rich right now, as well.

"Yeah, but hurry up before I change my mind," said Sophie, now more anxious than ever to feel some kind of high.

Tyrone led Sophie into his living room. He was pretty embarrassed by the looks of it. Ever since he starting smoking crack, he stopped caring about how he lived and didn't too much care about his appearance anymore either. He saw how Sophie looked at him when he answered the door. He used to have a major crush on her once upon a time, but Sophie would never give him any play. She was faithful to her husband. He wondered if she was still married to him. He quickly removed those thoughts from his mind. There was no way that she would want him now, just by seeing how her face twisted up when she saw how he was living.

"You need to get a cleaning lady in here, Tyrone," she said. Sophie was absolutely disgusted by the dingy furniture and all of the mess that surrounded it. When she spotted a cockroach crawl beneath the coffee table, she knew that she had to hurry up and get out of there.

She hadn't seen a roach since she was about five years old.

"I know. I've been kind of busy lately. I don't really be here anyway," Tyrone said with embarrassment. "Anyway, sit down and I'll get the equipment."

Sophie sat on the edge of the couch and tried to get her mind off of the roach, but after Brian kept reappearing in her thoughts, she decided to direct her attention back to that roach. As a matter of fact, that roach reminded her of Brian. No matter how hard she tried to get rid of him, he would keep coming back. Sophie jumped when Tyrone entered the living room. "You scared me."

"Sorry. Didn't mean to scare you. You must have a lot on your mind. Don't worry, this shit right here is the cure to all problems."

That was exactly what Sophie wanted to hear because she hoped to get a good night's sleep later that evening. She hadn't slept well since the incident at Rita's club. She still could not believe that Brian hit her the way he did. It was hard for her to get that image out of her head. And now, with Brian's dangerous behavior towards her, she knew that it would be even more difficult to rest. She dreaded going home, but she would be damned if she couldn't get any peace in her own house. She would find a way to get rid of Brian on her own.

"Okay, here is the pipe," Tyrone said. "All you gotta do is place this rock in this hole, take a lighter and light the bottom of it, and then put your mouth right here. But don't inhale it too fast. Start off with just a little and see how you like it before you hit it again."

Sophie was hesitant at first. She'd seen this on television and heard stories about people being hooked on drugs, and it wasn't anything nice. But that was them, and she wouldn't be like them. She just needed to get through this one night.

Tyrone watched Sophie as she place the rock into the pipe and followed his instructions. He wanted to scream at her to stop. He didn't want her to turn into what he had become. She had always been so nice to him. But the dollar signs flashed in his eyes as he watched her inhale her first hit of the poison.

"Oh, shit! Oh, shit! Oh, shit!" Sophie screamed. She could hardly breathe at first but all of a sudden, she was more relaxed than she had ever been in her life. She laid her head back on the couch, no longer caring about the roaches or Brian. She smiled at the stars that were starting to form before her eyes. *"This is some good stuff,"* she thought. *"Some very good stuff!"*

Tyrone knew what she was feeling. The first hit was always the best. And what Sophie didn't realize was that she would be chasing that first high over and over again.

* * * *

Chapter 23

"*While Sophie was experiencing the best high of her life, Brian nervously awaited for her arrival. "I hope she didn't take me serious when I said I would hurt her mother. I know I've been acting crazy lately, but what else can I do? I am not going to wind up homeless like some old bum. I gotta do what I gotta do for now. Sorry pops! I guess I am just like you."*

Just then the house alarm went off, scaring Brian half to death. Brian jumped from the bed and rushed into the front of the house ready for the confrontation. *"What if Sophie sent someone here to kick my ass?"* he thought. Just as he was reaching for the lamp to use as a weapon, whomever triggered the alarm stumbled over, landed flat on their face and started to laugh. The sound of the laughter was familiar, and that was when Brian saw Sophie lying flat on her face. "What are you doing?" he asked. She was starting to scare him.

Sophie picked herself up from the floor and walked to Brian. "Hey, baby!" she slurred.

Brian was confused by Sophie's new attitude. "Hey," he said nervously. There was definitely something going on with her. *"She must have started to smoke weed again,"* he thought.

Sophie smiled at her man. "Now, what was it that you needed from me?" she asked.

"What in the world is wrong with her?" Brian thought. But he supposed that this was exactly how he wanted her, especially after she messed up his chances of getting the fifty grand from Rita. Brian took advantage of the moment. "I want you to help me get my business started," he said.

Sophie continued to feel the effects of the cocaine. She felt daring. More daring than she had ever felt in her life. "How much?" she asked.

"Seventy-Five Thousand," Brian said almost in a whisper. He figured that since she was being so generous, an extra twenty-five grand would help him out even more.

"Seventy-Five? Is that all? How about One Hundred? Or, maybe I should give you a million?" Sophie began to laugh again. She laughed so hard that she dropped to the floor not being able to control it.

Brian was appalled and embarrassed. *So, she trying to make a fool out of me!* He didn't find it funny, not funny at all. The same rage that he felt earlier that day returned within him. Brian kicked his leg back as far as he could and then swung it directly at Sophie's head.

Sophie never saw Brian's feet coming at her, but when she finally came to, she felt the right side of her face thumping with pain. When she looked up, Brian was standing over her. Her high was definitely gone now. She only felt the pain of her right eye beginning to swell and that pissed her off more than anything. "You mother fucker!" she screamed as she got up and charged at Brian.

Brian jumped back as Sophie wildly swung her arms, scratching him a few times on his face. *This girl is nuts!* Brian caught Sophie by both of her wrists and pushed her up against the wall.

Sophie cried out desperately. "Why are you doing this to me? Why! Why! Whyyyyyyyyyyyyyyyy!"

Her cries actually put a little guilt in Brian's heart. *Why am I doing this to her? Why pops? What does this shit prove?* He let go of Sophie's wrists and stepped a few feet away from her. "Look, Sophie. Let's just stop all of this craziness. I don't have anywhere to go right now and all I'm asking is for a little help. I'll pay you back every penny. I'm sorry for hurting...."

"Fuck you!" Sophie interrupted. "I'm not giving you shit, you...."

"See! I'm trying to be nice and look at how you're talking to me! Fuck me! No, fuck you!" There was no point in even trying to change. He'd get more out of the deal if he kept the fear in her. He no longer cared anymore. He was going to start his construction business soon and no one was going to stop him. "Tomorrow morning," he said, "if I don't see a check made out to me for $75,000, then you can kiss your poor mother goodbye!"

"And if I do? Then what!" Sophie screamed. "Are you then going to leave my house!"

"I can tell you this, if you keep your mouth shut and go along with what I have to do, then you won't have anything to worry about," Brian said. He wanted to get away from her as well, but not until he got more out of it.

Sophie gave up. She didn't want her mother to be in danger. Without her mother, Sophie knew she wouldn't survive. She was glad that she had nine more bags of crack to get her through the remaining days with Brian, and then after he left, she would never have to smoke another one. She refused to be anybody's crackhead.

Ding dong! Ding dong!

The sound of the doorbell startled both Brian and Sophie. "Who in the hell is this coming over here at this hour?" Brian asked.

Sophie walked over to the intercom and tried to keep her tone at a calm level. "Who is it?"

"It's your mother! Open the gates!" Paulette screamed.

Brian heard the voice of the unwelcomed guest. He warned Sophie again. "Remember what I said! Go and clean yourself up. I'll open the door for her!" Brian knew that Paulette didn't like him and frankly, he didn't care. He knew he wouldn't hurt the old woman, but if he had to, he didn't think it would effect him mentally. He was starting to hate her too.

Sophie obeyed Brian. She knew her eye was more swollen than before because she could hardly see her way to the bathroom. She looked in the mirror and her once upon a time beautiful face looked like that of a monster. She cried at her reflection. *Why is this happening to me?* Sophie took one of her magic rocks and placed it into the glass pipe. She choked off the first hit but the second one went down smoothly. She then sat on the toilet and let the high take its effect. "*Damn, this stuff is amazing,*" she sang.

* * * *

Chapter 24

"How are you today, Paulette?" Brian asked trying to control his nervousness.

"Where is my daughter?" Paulette asked purposely ignoring Brian's greeting.

"She's in the bathroom. She had a little accident."

"What kind of accident?" Paulette asked full of concern for her only daughter.

"She um, well, she….."

Sophie exited the bathroom with a horrendous black eye and a huge smile on her face. "Mother!" she sang. "How are you this evening?"

"Your eye! What happened to your eye!" Paulette ran over to Sophie to inspect the damage.

She then whipped her head at Brian. "What did you do to her?"

Brian froze.

"Nothing, mother!" Sophie interrupted. "Brian has nothing to do with this. I slipped when I came in the door earlier." Sophie shocked both Brian and his mother when she started to giggle, and even more when her giggles turned into uncontrollable laughter.

"Sophie, are you drunk?" her mother asked.

"No....I'm....not.....drunk!" she slurred.

Paulette grabbed her daughter's face. She didn't smell any alcohol on her daughter's breath, but there was an unfamiliar smell surrounding her. *"Maybe it was some sort of medicine that Sophie put on her eye,"* she thought. "Baby, you're acting really strange. Are you sure you're alright? What happened to your eye?"

"She already told you," Brian interrupted. "She fell down when..."

"I am not speaking to you! My daughter can speak for herself!" Paulette said angrily. That was when she noticed the scratches and a couple of bruises on Brian's face. "And I suppose you slipped and fell also?"

"What are you talking about?" Brian asked. He knew that Sophie scratched him a few times, but didn't think that they or the bruises from the fight with the guy from Rita's poetry club were too noticeable.

"Mother, I don't appreciate you talking to my man like that!" Sophie screamed. "If you don't mind, Brian and I were just getting ready for bed. I'll call you in the morning."

Paulette was speechless. She knew something terrible had just happened to her daughter. And her daughter was protecting this man. But why? She didn't want to make the matter any worse so she presented a phony smile. "Okay. I'll leave then. Sophie, baby, you be sure to give me a call tomorrow, okay? I love you baby."

"I love you too, ma!" Sophie screamed just a little too loud and proud.

Brian and Paulette both stared at her.

Paulette cleared her throat and walked towards the front door. "Good night." By the time she reached her car, she was overwhelmed with emotion. *What is that boy doing to my baby?*

Chapter 25

"That's great news, Charles. "I'm glad we're able to open the club again tomorrow. I've been receiving lots of telephone calls from our regulars asking about the reopening."

"Yeah, me too. We have to make sure another incident like that never happens again," said Charles. "How's that eye?"

"Swelling went down....."

"That's good to hear. Have you heard from any one of them?" he asked.

"Yeah, Ms. Ignorant showed up at my house earlier this evening asking for my help to get rid of Brian."

"What do you mean by getting rid of him?"

"Well, I think he hit her or something and now she's scared."

Charles was confused. "You *think* he hit her? Well, did he or not?"

"I believe so. She also mentioned something about him threatening to hurt her mother if she told anyone."

"Rita, I'm getting more confused here. What exactly was it that she wanted from you? Tell me about your conversation with her."

"There's really nothing to tell. I didn't talk to her really. She was screaming through my front door trying to get me to talk to her. She wanted me to give her more information about Brian so that she could figure out how to get out of the relationship."

"And you didn't?" Charles asked.

"No. There is really no information to give, but I guess I could have given her his mother's information. I felt bad for her, but I just didn't want to help her out."

"Why?"

"I don't know. I guess I'm still upset about the incident at the club."

"So, if the shoe were on the other foot, would you have wanted someone to do you that way?"

"No, I guess not, but that's life." I was starting to become a bit tired of everyone's pity for Sophie. *What about me?* I wanted to scream, but instead decided to end our conversation. "Charles, I'll see you tomorrow. I have to get some rest for the reopening. Thanks, again."

"You're welcome. See you tomorrow then."

* * * *

Charles hung up the phone and had to shake off the fact that his friend, Rita, could be so cold-hearted. That terrified him even more of asking her out on a date.

* * * *

Chapter 26
Eight Months Later

"You wouldn't believe who I saw walking up Blue Island Road the other night at 3:00 in the morning!" said Tish.

Jackie squinted her eyes at Tish. "I'm not even going to ask why you were out until 3:00 in the morning. But who did you see?"

"Girl, I'm still young and I party until the club closes, you heard me?" said Tish as she did her best impression of a ghetto bootie dance.

"Who did you see?" asked an impatient Jackie.

"Sophie."

"Who?"

"You remember Sophie? Ahmad's ex-wife? The one who Rita had that fight with about a year ago?"

"Oh, yeah. Is she still dating Brian?"

"I don't know, but I know she was looking really bad."

"What do you mean by bad?"

"Girl, her hair was unkempt, clothes were wrinkled and she didn't have on any makeup."

"Damn, I have never known Sophie to not take care of herself. I wonder what's going on with her," said Jackie. "I still never forgave Rita for not helping that poor girl, but you know how she is. I think I might make a surprise trip over to Sophie's to see if she's okay. I feel bad about losing touch with her after her divorce. Ahmad was more my friend than she was, but that's still no excuse for cutting her off. Maybe Rita will go with me."

Tish looked through the glass panes of the restaurant and saw Rita. "Speak of the devil, here she comes."

* * * *

I walked into the restaurant with diva confidence. I sported my red business suit, which in my opinion, represented power. Charles loved when I wore it. Of all the men who walked into my life, I never figured I'd wind up with Charles. Turns out, he always had a secret crush on me, but I was always too busy to notice. When he asked me out on a date, I was shocked, but didn't turn him down. We have been dating ever since and my old lonely boring life turned into one filled with love and happiness.

I was running a little late with meeting the girls for our Sunday brunch. "Hey ladies. Sorry I'm late. Late night with Charles again."

"You two still at it again? You need to come up for air more often, chickee," said Tish. "You two really make a great couple. How long has it been?"

"Six months. Can you believe that?"

"That's great girl. And you seem so happy," said Tish.

"Yes, I am. If I had known that he was a perfect gentleman, I would have hooked up with him a long time ago."

Jackie looked at her friend and noticed how happy she has been lately. She didn't want to spoil her friend's good spirits, but she couldn't get Sophie out of her mind. "Rita, can I ask you a question?"

"You just did."

"What?"

"Now that's two questions," Rita said.

"Jackie, you are so slow," Tish said as her and Rita laughed at their inside joke.

"Whatever," said Jackie. "I was wondering if you wanted to go and visit Sophie with me next week. Tish was just telling me how bad she was looking the other night."

"Sophie! Girl, I'm not going to go and see that crackhead."

"Crackhead!" Jackie screamed. "Sophie's on drugs now?"

"You didn't hear? A girl that hangs out at my club told me that she sees her at some dude named Tyrone's house damn near every week. Tyrone is a crack dealer and he's Sophie's supplier."

"Why didn't you tell me?" Jackie was now upset with her friend for not relaying that information to her.

"Because Sophie and Brian are in my past! I'm not looking back anymore! What happens with them is none of my business, although people around town love to update me on the Sophie and Brian story every chance they get."

Jackie knew that Rita had a point, but she couldn't let the subject go that easily. "Is she still with Brian?"

No matter how long ago my relationship with Brian ended, I couldn't get away from it. "I don't want to talk about it, okay?"

"Rita, please! I'm concerned for her, that's all. She was never the type to get hooked on drugs," Jackie pleaded.

I couldn't take anymore of everyone sympathizing for Sophie. Eight months later and still, I couldn't get away from Brian and Sophie. "If you're so concerned about her, then why don't you go over there yourself and talk to her, instead of keeping me in their business? I'm tired of everybody hounding me about her. Even Charles keeps telling me how wrong I was. Damn! Can I get a break from this shit?"

"I'm sorry, Rita!" Jackie said. "I didn't know you felt that way about helping someone out! Tish, I'll talk to you later. I'm outta here!"

"Jackie, wait!" I hollered. "Jackie!"

Tish was speechless. She didn't know who's side to be on. Both ladies had a point. "Everything will work itself out," she said to me. "Everything will be fine."

* * *

Chapter 27

"Slow down there, Sophie!" Tyrone was starting to get just a little tired of Sophie hanging around his apartment every day. She had been coming by at the same time everyday for two months. He knew that she would become hooked on the drugs, but never in a million years did he think that she would live for them. She used to be such a fine woman; now she looked like your everyday crackhead. "Give me some of that, girl! You know you have to pass the shit around!" Tyrone said as he snatched the crack-filled pipe from Sophie's hand.

"Damn, Tyrone! I'm not as high as I'd like to be right now," Sophie said as she laid her head back against the dingy pillow.

"How high are you trying to get? You smoked half of it! And besides, what the hell you trying to get real high for? Don't you have a man at home waiting for you?"

"Ha! What man!"

"The one you run home to everyday when you come from over here, that's who?"

"If that's what you want to call him. A man, puhleeze…try more like a little boy."

"If he's all that bad, then why don't you get rid of him?"

"It's not that easy."

"What do you mean? Shit, aint that your crib?"

"Yeah, but it's more difficult than you think."

"How's that?"

Her high was starting to kick in as she daydreamed about her abusive relationship. She'd never confided in Tyrone before; she never confided in anyone, but for some reason, she knew she had to talk about it or she was going to go even crazier. And at the moment, Tyrone was her only friend. "Do you really want to hear my story, Ty?"

"Yeah, why not?"

"Okay, but if I tell you, you have to promise me one thing."

"Anything."

"Just promise me that you won't reveal what I'm going to tell you to anybody, okay?"

"Okay…, but damn, is it that bad?"

"Yeah, it's pretty bad," Sophie said as she laid back to enjoy her high, contemplating how to start her story.

Sophie told Tyrone of all of the beatings Brian gave her whenever she denied him her car or money. She recalled one day when Brian wanted to run up to the local grocery store to buy a couple of junk food items, but had not a penny in his wallet. He asked her for the money, but she denied him. Although it was just a few bucks, Sophie was sick and tired of giving Brian her money. He'd refuse to look for a job. She told him that she wouldn't give him another dime and that was when Brian went nuts and started to beat her up and down her very own living room. It was after that incident that Sophie knew that Brian's abuse was not just a little problem. After that incident, it had gotten worse. There would be not a day that went by that Brian didn't hit her. He'd threaten to kill her a couple of times also. She told Tyrone of one time when Brian knocked out one of her teeth because she denied him her car keys. She turned her back for just one second and before she knew it, POW! His fist hit her so hard that she blacked out for a minute.

That was the reason she didn't bother trying to look good anymore. It seemed that the better she looked, the more Brian wanted to ruin her beauty. The only downfall to not looking her best, was that Brian wouldn't dare touch her in the bedroom and in Sophie's opinion, that was the only good out of the relationship.

"Damn," was all Tyrone could say.

"Yeah, I know," Sophie said as she giggled.

"Aint nothing funny about that shit, Sophie," Tyrone said.

"I know. I'm just real high right now," she said. "Well, anyway, after the incidents with the beatings, I just couldn't take it anymore, so I just started giving in to everything. Everything he wanted, I gave to him. That man has spent over $300,000 of my money already!"

"Damn, you got that much money, girl?"

"Slow your roll, man," Sophie said. I only have enough for one man to spend. Don't go trying to join him," she laughed.

"Well, what are you going to do? You're just going to let that man spend up all your money like that?" Tyrone asked.

"Ty, I really don't care anymore. I don't care about shit. As far as I'm concerned, he can have it all, as long as he leaves me enough to keep this damn habit I picked up."

"You don't blame me for that, do you?" Tyrone asked feeling guiltier than ever. Every time he saw Sophie, he felt terrible about selling her that first rock. He wished that he could have turned back the clock, but during those times, he needed every penny he could get.

"No, I don't blame you. I blame him. Shit, besides, if it wasn't for you, I would have killed myself a long time ago."

"Well, you are killing yourself slowly right now. This shit aint no good for you," he said.

"Hell, to be honest with you, Ty, I don't care too much about living. How could I ever get myself back? The only thing that ever kept me happy before this habit was my husband, Ahmad. But to be totally honest with you, I don't think he loved me like I thought he did. Everyone who I come in contact with always seem to hurt me. I've never been truly happy. The only person I have is my mother and I think even she's ashamed of me right now. She knows something is going on with me, but she can't quite put her finger on it. Every time she asks me if there was something I want to tell her, I'd just laugh it off. She would disown me if she ever found out the truth about what I'm doing to myself!"

"Sophie, I think you're being too hard on yourself. Why don't you just get him out of there and get some police protection…then get yourself into a rehab and reclaim your life."

"It's not that easy, Ty. Shit, he threatened to hurt my mother if I ever called the police on him."

"Look, girl. I know some people who would gladly get rid of him for you, for the perfect price."

"What are you saying, that I should have him killed?"

"From what you telling me, I'm surprised you didn't have him killed a long time ago!"

"No, thanks, Ty. You may think I'm stupid for saying this, but since my divorce, I've been a little on the lonely side, and Brian….well, Brian sort of makes up for me not having to come home to an empty house."

Tyrone couldn't believe his ears. "Yeah, you do sound stupid", he said. "You also sound confused. You basically just said that you hate him and now you're saying that he makes up for you not having to be alone. I never understood women like you."

"Hell, I don't understand myself right now," said Sophie.

Can I ask you a question, Sophie?"

"Shoot."

"Sophie, you used to be or shall I say, you are such an attractive lady who could get any man she wanted, do you think that Brian was the best you could do?"

"Ty, because I am not a socialite, it's hard for me to meet guys. I don't have any girlfriends, and it's hard to meet men when the only person you hang with is your mother."

"So, go out there and meet some girlfriends, then."

"I've never been good at meeting people, Ty. So, let's just let it be. Brian will change one day, I hope. Now, pass that pipe over here."

Tyrone let the subject go. There was nothing he could say to someone as stubborn as Sophie. He handed her the clear glass full of poison. "Sophie, just so you know, I'm going into a rehab tomorrow, which means that I aint going to be selling this shit no more after tonight."

Sophie panicked. "What!…..Who can I get it……What am I suppose to do?…"

"I don't know, girl. But if I were you, I'd consider joining me. You need a lot of help and if you want, I'll see if I could get you in too."

"No…no….no…..I'm not ready yet. What do you have left? Just give me what you got left, then!"

"All I got left is this bag full. It's worth two grand, but I don't want to sell it to you. You need to get with the program and come in with me."

"I will, soon, okay? Just let me write you a check for it. The check is good, I promise."

"You buying the whole thing?"

"Yeah, I need it." Sophie reached down for her purse and wrote out a check to give to Tyrone. She envied the fact that he was trying to better his life, but she wasn't willing to let go of the very thing that kept her on the sane side.

Tyrone shook his head in utter disappointment as Sophie handed him a check for $2,000.00.

Chapter 28

When the house alarm went off at 1:30 in the morning, Brian knew not to get up. For the past couple of months, Sophie had no concept of time. He'd found drug paraphernalia hidden underneath the hood of the toilet and also noticed Sophie's new generous attitude. Sophie finally gave in and had given him access to most of her bank accounts. When she gave him his very own checkbook to withdraw money, Brian knew it had to be the drugs. Not only did he get the $75,000 he asked for, but also more clothing, jewelry and the car of his dreams.

He tried to remain in deep denial of Sophie's drug habit; he would hate to think it was him to cause her to turn to such a deadly drug. He tried to retain in his mind that Sophie had been on that stuff before he met her, only he didn't know. At any rate, he would be gone soon. He'd set the deal with PRC Construction to buy them out. It would only be a few more months until the deal closed, then he would leave Sophie and let her get her life back on track. He wanted to care more for her, but he didn't. He did have to admit to himself that Sophie had been the jackpot of his life and he would always be grateful for her.

Sophie stumbled into the bedroom. "Hey, are you woke?"

Brian pretended to be asleep. He knew what she wanted and he didn't want to give it to her. She had been begging for him to sleep with her for the last two months now and he couldn't. He didn't like looking at her. Those drugs were eating her alive.

"Brian. Sp……sp……sp……….. wake up!"

"What Sophie?" Brian said agitatedly.

"Hey. How about a little nookie tonight? Please?"

"No."

"Why?"

"Because I'm tired."

"Come on, please?" begged Sophie.

"I said no!"

"You don't love me anymore?"

"Yeah, yeah, yeah, I do. I'm just tired right now! Go and take a shower, you stink!"

"What!"

"I said you stink! Which crackhouse did you go to tonight?"

Sophie was embarrassed. She had no idea that Brian knew what she had been up to. "What are you talking about, Brian?" she asked.

"Sophie, I'm not stupid. How long have you been on that stuff?" Brian asked.

"What stuff?"

"So now you want to play stupid? The cocaine! How long, Sophie?"

Sophie chewed down on her nails. She never expected to be questioned by Brian. She thought that her secret was safe. Not even her mother could figure out what was going on with her, notwithstanding the fact that she hadn't seen her mother in a few months. Paulette called her mostly everyday to see how she was doing. Sophie always pepped up her voice so that her mother wouldn't worry so much about her. "Brian, I don't know what to say. I'm so embarrassed."

Brian startled Sophie when he jumped out of the bed and screamed at her. "You should be! If I had known that you were on that shit, I never would have been with you in the first place!"

"What! I can't believe you said that! It's because of you that I'm on this shit! It's because of you that I can't get off of this shit! It's all your fault!"

That was what Brian did not want to hear. "My fault? How? I didn't sell that shit to you! How is it my fault?"

"Because you have mentally drained me, Brian! You demanded money, I gave it to you. You demanded that I stop going over to my mom's, I did that for you! I tried to tell you that I didn't want you, then you beat me up! That's why I'm on this shit! That's why!" Sophie broke down in tears.

He knew he didn't love Sophie, but he hated to see her this way. She smelled of mildew, her hair was falling out, her teeth were no longer white and she had dropped at least 50 pounds in the last couple of months. He refused to believe it was him who caused her to turn to drugs. "Don't blame me for your problems, Sophie. It was you who caused me and Rita to...."

Sophie interrupted. "Don't!" she screamed. "I'm tired of you trying to make me feel guilty about you and Rita breaking up! How many fucking times are you going to drill that in my head, huh? Yes, I broke you up! Big fucking deal! I wish someone would come in here and take your ass away from me!"

"Okay, I'll leave, then. First thing in the morning."

Sophie's cry immediately stopped. "What?"

"You heard me. I'll leave in the morning!"

"You're leaving me now? After the beatings? After I turned to drugs? After you damn near drained my bank accounts? Why now?"

"Didn't you just say that you wanted someone to take me away? Well, you got your wish. My company will be up and running soon and then I'll pay you back!"

"So, you finally got what you wanted, huh? Fine! I'm glad I could help!"

Sophie didn't want to be left alone. Not now! How could she ever face her mother again? How could she ever pick herself back up? She was addicted to crack cocaine now and she didn't feel that she would ever be able to kick the habit. The drugs were the only escape for her pain. It made her feel so damn good. So damn free!

Brian walked over to Sophie and she flinched, thinking that she was going to receive yet another unnecessary beating. "I'm not going to hit you. I just wanted to know if there is anything I could do to help you. I know plenty of drug rehabs I can direct you to."

"I'm not going to anybody's damn rehab! I'm going to be fine!"

"Sophie, you need to get help!"

"What I needed Brian, was to never have let you into my life! If anybody needs help, it is you! You've destroyed me and now it's too late to try and be concerned."

Brian felt horrible. Flashes of his father appeared before his eyes. He was worse than his father. At least his father never caused his mother to turn to drugs. "I'm sorry."

Sophie laughed. "You're sorry? You're sorry! After eight months of beatdowns and being held hostage in my own house, you're sorry now?"

This time it was Brian who broke down and there was nothing phony about it. "Sophie, I'm a fuck up! I've always been a fuck up! You're right, I do need help! Brian got up and started to pack his things while the tears fell like waterfalls down his cheeks. Look, I gotta go. I'll leave tonight. I'm sorry for what I put you through."

"I can't believe you, Brian! I can't belieeeeeeve this!" she screamed. "If you are so damn sorry, then why don't you leave all of the money I gave you on the table! Leave everything you used me for! How about that!"

"I can't," he cried. "It's not that easy! I'll pay you back every penny, I promise."

"You also promised to make me happy! And all you've given me were beat-downs and receipts! You used me and you used Rita! I figured that out a long time ago!"

"You're right! I did use you both. That's not how I want to be! Do you think I enjoy this? Well, I don't!"

Sophie went into the top drawer and pulled out a blade, together with a bag full of cocaine. "Do you think I enjoy doing this, huh?" She poured the cocaine over the top of the drawer and started to divide it into several lines. Once she sectioned it all off, she sniffed a long line into her nostrils."

"Sophie, don't do that! Don't!" Brian screamed.

"This is the only thing that keeps me sane enough to keep coming home to you!" Then,

Sophie took in the second line. "I hate you and everything you've done to me!" she said as she took in the third line. She continued to take it all in her nose until blood started to seep from her nose and the corner of her mouth. "You can take everything, you bastard! "I'm sorry momma!" she cried. "I'm sorry Ahmad! I hate you Brian! Oh, God! Look at me! Look at what you've done to me, Brian!"

Brian was in shock. He couldn't move. Sophie was going crazy right before his eyes. She had the white powder all over her face, hair and clothing. He felt as if he was watching a movie – this could not be real. When Sophie fell over into a seizure, his legs went limp.

"Sophie! Sophie! Get up!" he screamed.

Panic set in and Brian's life flashed before his eyes as if he were the one who overdosed. His hands were shaking so badly, he could hardly dial 9-1-1. "I need help now! She's overdosing! Help!" he cried into the receiver.

Chapter 29

I had to make amends with my best friend. It had been two months since I last saw Jackie. I couldn't stand seeing her so upset with me. I banged on her door. "Jackie, open up, it's me, Rita!"

Jackie opened the door and gave me a disappointing look. "What do you want, Rita?"

"I came over to apologize to you. I'm sorry about the other day."

"I'm not the one you should apologize to."

"I know, Jackie. You're right. It's just that this past year has been so drama free. I'm sorry I didn't tell you about Sophie being on drugs. I just wanted them to remain in the past. I went through a lot with Brian too, but I guess I got upset because it seemed like you were more concerned for Sophie than you were me."

"Rita, you are my best friend and I'll always care about you. The difference between you and Sophie is that you're stronger. Now look at Sophie. She's out there all strung out because of a man that you should have told her about, regardless of what she's done to you."

Boy did Jackie bring back all of the guilt that I've been trying to hide. "You're right. Do you still want to go over and talk with Sophie? If so, I'm game."

"Of course, I do. She needs help!"

"Okay, let's go," I said. "Get dressed. I'll be in the car."

As I was heading to the car, I'd thought about my last encounter with Sophie. She seemed very frightened and all I did was turn her away. I felt ashamed by my actions. Whatever it took, I promised myself that no matter what, I would never ever turn my back on anyone else who needed me.

Jackie ran towards the car with her robe still on. "What's up girl, why aren't you dressed?"

"I just called over to Sophie's to let her know that we were on our way." Jackie was shaking. "Her mother answered the telephone…"

"And?"

"Rita, Sophie's dead!"

"What! Oh my God! Did Brian…"

"No. It wasn't Brian. She overdosed on cocaine!"

I couldn't breathe. The guilt! Oh the guilt! I started to curse myself for treating her so awful when she begged for my help. "It's my fault! It's my fault!"

Jackie ran over to comfort me. "No, it's not your fault, Rita. Don't blame yourself!"

"How could I not blame myself? If I would have told her about Brian from the get go, then she wouldn't be dead today! Oh my God!"

"No, Rita. It's not your fault. Please, come inside and we'll have a cup of tea," Jackie pleaded.

"No, I have to go. I'll call you later today, okay?"

"Are you going to be alright?" Jackie asked.

"Yes….I think so….." I turned the key to my ignition and headed home. I wanted to be alone to dwell in my misery. "Poor Sophie. What have I done?"

* * * *

Chapter 30

"You have to get out of bed, Rita," said Charles. "Sophie's death is not your fault! Please, baby, stop blaming yourself."

"I can't help it, sweetie. I feel so bad!" I said. "I don't know what to do!"

"Well you know how writing makes you feel better. Why don't you write a poem about your feelings on this matter. That should make you feel a little better."

"Charles, you have been such a sweetheart and I appreciate you trying to comfort me, but writing a poem is not going to change the fact that Sophie is dead. That could have been me! Maybe not the drugs, but he would have driven me crazy eventually if it weren't for Sophie taking him away."

"You can't keep going on like this, baby! To be honest with you, it's not Brian's fault either.

Sophie went to drugs because that was her decision. You don't know for a fact how long she's been into them. It may have been Brian who drove her crazy, but he didn't kill her. She killed herself."

"I know, Charles! She did kill herself, but do you think she would be dead if I helped her when she needed me?"

Charles didn't have an answer.

"That's what I thought." I said feeling guiltier than ever.

* * * *

Chapter 31

Faye comforted her son as he cried in her arms.

"She's dead! I'm a monster!" Brian cried.

Faye knew that her son's behavior would lead to something awful, but she had never imagined it leading to someone's death. She continued to hold her son as he spoke with Dr. Monroe, a licensed psychiatrist.

Dr. Monroe continued to write on his steno pad as he continued to ask more questions. "Brian, tell me what happened?" he asked.

"I used her, that's what happened! I took her money, threatened to hurt her mother if she told anyone what I was doing and beat her for no reason. I drove her to kill herself!"

"You blame yourself for her suicide?" he asked.

Brian gave the doctor a puzzled look. "I just told you, man! If I'd never done her that way, she'd still be alive today!"

"I see," said Dr. Monroe. Maybe she committed suicide to prove something to you – to make you feel bad about doing those things, but I don't think you should put the whole blame on yourself."

"Why not? She was happy before I came around," cried Brian.

"So you think that because you used her and beat her, that it lead to her committing suicide? Did you know of anything else in Sophie's past that could have caused her any misery?"

"All I know is that she went through a divorce."

"What happened with her marriage?"

"She caught him cheating on her."

"And how did you meet her?"

"At my girlfriend at the time's poetry club."

"Did she know that you were dating someone else when you met her?"

"Yes."

"And, what happened?"

"She wanted me anyway."

"Now, tell me why you blame yourself for her suicide?"

"I already told you! I was awful to her!"

"You just told me that she wanted you despite you having a girlfriend already. Do you think that maybe she was lonely and was trying to replace her husband? Or maybe the divorce was the true reason for her breakdown? There could be lots of reasons, but unfortunately, we will never know."

"Possibly. But her husband didn't do the things I did to her."

"That may be true. But first, I want you to stop blaming yourself for her suicide because you do not know Sophie's whole story. But what we want to start working on are the problems that *you* feel may have caused Sophie's suicide, like your temper. I want you to be serious about these sessions that are forthcoming. But first, I want you to repeat to yourself over and over again, that you do have a problem and that you really want help.

"I want to get help! I want to get help!" he cried.

Brian knew that his days of being a gigolo were over after seeing what Sophie did to herself, right before his eyes. When the police questioned him, he wanted to confess. He wanted to tell them that he killed her because that's how he felt, but still, he did not want to go to jail. Not now, not ever! But he knew he needed to get some kind of professional help and there was nothing that was going to make him change his mind this time. When the police asked him if he lived at Sophie's residence, he denied it; however, he did tell them that they were having relationship problems and that was what led to her suicide. When he was released from questioning, he never returned to Sophie's house. He left everything, including the checkbooks and credit cards. He also made a call to PRC Construction and all of its lawyers, as well as his lawyer, and terminated the purchase deal, also asking them to return the money to Sophie's accounts. He no longer cared about owning his own construction business, all he wanted to do now was grow up and finally become his own man. He just hated the fact that it took the death of a beautiful woman to finally wake him up.

* * * *

Chapter 32

After Sophie's funeral, I went over to the club. Charles wanted to escort me to the funeral, but I wanted to do it alone. When he saw me walk in the club, he ran over to see how I was doing.

"Are you okay?" he asked.

"I think so. I freaked out in front of her mother though."

"That's understandable, baby. You've been through a lot. Let me get you a drink."

"No, a drink won't be necessary. Who's up next?"

"Maxximus is up. I know how much you love his poetry. Do you want me to tell him to recite something that will cheer you up?"

"Maybe later. But first, why don't you introduce me. I wrote something on my way over here that I would like to share."

"You did? That's wonderful, Rita. I can't wait to hear it."

I smiled. Charles was such a great man. I gave my new future husband a kiss and thanked him for always being there for me.

"Anytime, Rita. I love you," he said.

Charles walked onto the stage to introduce me as the next poet. The audience applauded. I walked up in my black dress, black hat and pained heart to recite my poem. "I wrote this poem for a sista who needed me .... Anyway, here it is..."

Paulette walked in the door as I started to recite my poem. She smiled at me with such sweetness. That brought more tears to my eyes. I didn't think she remembered me at the funeral, but I suppose she figured it out after I left. I continued with my poem, *Apology From One Sista' To Another:*

> *I apologize for my angers towards you*
> *when I accused you of stealing my man*
> *I can't imagine the things you went through and I'm sorry*
> *that I thanked you for taking him off my hands*
>
> *I apologize for the curses I put on you*
> *I was a little jealous I must admit*
> *But when Brian walked out of my life*
> *It made it hard for me to commit*
>
> *I hated all men for what he did to me*
> *That man almost ruined my life*
> *I did pray for you everyday though*
> *I hope that makes things between us alright*

Apology From One Sista' To Another

I apologize for not warning you
About my ex-man's temper and rage
And I'm sorry that I didn't explain to you
That he was dangerous and that's why I couldn't get away

I apologize for calling you those awful names
When I pushed you and spit in your face
I'm sorry for yelling at you on the phone
Telling you that he was mine and please, stay away

I apologize for hearing the rumors
and not wanting to get involved
I would have told you that he was a man
who never knew how to love

See, Brian was the type of man who only wanted you
for the purpose of having power
Hour after hour I used to cry
because I was afraid of him – a big coward!

I always thought that Brian would go back
to the man he was before
And I knew he was giving you that special treatment
but only to get inside your door

I felt sorry for the life Brian had in store for you
I knew his love for you would fade
I knew deep down you wouldn't be happy for long
But my instincts told me to stay away

So I hope one day you'll accept my apology
Soon one day we'll speak
I'm very sorry for what he did to you
MAY YOU REST IN PEACE

Paulette walked on the stage and gave me one of the best hugs I'd ever received, one that reminded me of my mother's.

"It's going to be alright, baby. It's all going to be fine. She forgives you. I know my baby, and she forgives you." We both broke down and cried our hearts out for the loss of Sophie Scott-Roberts. May God bless her soul.